CW00447989

Credits:

Edited by Mollie Traver and Linda Ingmanson

Cover Design by Deranged Doctor Design

ALEX LIDELL

GREAT FALLS ACADEMY

1: RULES OF STONE

ALSO BY ALEX LIDELL

New Adult Fantasy Romance

POWER OF FIVE (Reverse Harem Fantasy)

POWER OF FIVE

MISTAKE OF MAGIC

TRIAL OF THREE

LERA OF LUNOS

GREAT FALLS ACADEMY (Power of Five world)

RULES OF STONE

CRIME AND PUNISHMENT

SCENT OF A WOLF

Young Adult Fantasy Novels

TIDES

FIRST COMMAND (Prequel Novella)

AIR AND ASH

WAR AND WIND

SEA AND SAND

SCOUT

TRACING SHADOWS

UNRAVELING DARKNESS

TILDOR

THE CADET OF TILDOR

To my readers,

While drafting Great Falls Academy, I've received some wonderful questions. As you embark on this adventure with Lera, allow me to address some of the most frequent inquiries.

Why is Great Falls Academy told in an episode (novella) format instead of as a traditional novel series?

Episodes are a different way of telling a story. When logging into Netflix lately, I've found myself gravitating toward watching episode-based shows instead of choosing full-length films. Since I enjoy watching this type of media, I decided to explore it with my story telling in *Great Falls Academy*. Think *Buffy the Vampire Slayer* television series with fae. The episodes - novellas - will be released at regular intervals, each with an internal story and an over all season arc.

How does GREAT FALLS ACADEMY relate to the POWER OF FIVE series?

The events in GREAT FALLS ACADEMY take place about six months after the conclusion of the POWER OF FIVE series and feature the same main characters - Lera, River, Coal, Shade and Tye.

That said, the two story sets are independent, so reading one is not required to enjoy the other. Within the GREAT FALLS series, the episodes should be read in order.

Why Reverse Harem romance?

In Reverse Harem romances, the heroine forms romantic bonds with multiple heroes without ever having to chose one, as she would in a love-triangle scenario. In Lera's case, she is mated with four elite fae warriors. I've fallen in love with this genre because it provides the opportunity to explore four relationships within a single overarching world setting and plot. This gives me the leeway to go deeper into the characters and the story, while still giving a lot of screen time to the romance. Since I write fantasy—which requires a good deal of world building—this is especially nice.

Plus, #whychoose? :)

And now, whether this is your first taste of Lunos or Reverse Harem romance, or whether you are an experienced fan who knows all about the coming journey, curl up in your favorite chair and escape with Lera into Great Falls Academy.

Love,

Alex

LERA

"Watch your left side, mortal." Coal calls to me from where he fights three sclices at once, the fae warrior's sword and dagger a blur of precision. His voice is steady and low, as if we are in a practice corral facing nothing more deadly than sacks of sand.

"I'm. Not. Mortal." Unlike Coal's words, mine come between gasping breaths. My lungs burn, my heart pounding against my ribs as I spin, my sword following the arc of my body to bite into a sclice's thick hide.

The hoglike beast swipes at me with its clawed front limbs, which are long enough to let it run on all fours. It's not running now, though. Standing upright on its back-hinged hind legs, the sclice towers over me, its vertical red eyes, snouted nose, and fang-filled protruding lower jaw all roaring their displeasure.

"Keep leaving your weak side open, and we'll see how not mortal you are," Coal calls, felling the beast before him. In black fighting leathers, his blond hair pulled back with a leather thong, the warrior moves with a preternatural grace that comes of centuries of combat—and still takes my breath. A flick of his powerful forearm, and a second hog beast falls just as it tries to sink its teeth into Coal's shoulder.

Jumping away from the sclice's assault, I force myself to draw a lungful of air. My new immortal body might make me stronger and swifter than I was in my human form, but I've a ways to go before I can match skills with my mates.

I'm not mortal. The words still zing through me, settling uncomfortably into my bones. Only eight months ago, I was working in Master Zake's stable in the mortal lands, with nothing but the bite of his belt and the snap of his temper a reliable promise of the future. When the four fae warriors—Coal, River, Shade, and Tye—appeared from the immortal realm, drawn to me by an ancient magic, none believed our connection was anything but an error. And yet, here I am. Not just the fifth warrior of the quint, but fae myself, mated to all four males by a magic as old as the immortal race.

Now that we're a sanctioned quint, we're charged with protecting Lunos from the dark creatures of Mors—which, if it were up to Coal, would mean roving the lands between the three Lunos courts, Flury, Blaze, and Slait, and battling sclices and piranhas to his heart's content.

Unfortunately for Coal, because our commander is also now the king of Slait Court, we never travel far from Slait's capital. The males put on a good front, but after centuries on the front lines, responding to routine reports and checking wards make my males feel like leashed dogs.

Twenty paces away, where the thick fern forest gives way to a clearing, said commander, River, stands with his back straight and eyes narrowed in concentration as his magic opens a great gash in the frost-chilled earth. A future grave for the sclice pack that Tye and Shade herd into the crack while Coal and I deal with the strays. Sclices might have the brains and instincts of rodents, but with their man-sized bodies and insatiable hunger, large packs like this can destroy a village in a night's hunt.

I mark Shade, in his wolf form, snapping at the beasts' hind legs while red-haired Tye plays his fire magic to set off sparks beside their hooves. Swift. Efficient... Competitive. *Stars.* The two have made a game of it, and I'd wager my horse they are keeping score.

The sclice before me snarls its fury, thick yellow drool dripping from its pulled-back lips. The stench coming off the creature is strong enough to make me gag, even here in the Gloom—the normal world's eerie underlining, where Mors beasts tend to congregate—which mutes the colors and smells and sounds. Gripping my sword tighter, I cover my mouth and nose with my elbow as I circle for a better angle.

The hog beast crouches on its hind legs. Growls. Lunges at me faster than I thought possible, sharp front claws pushing off the ground for leverage before raking my left side. Streaks of fire light along my ribs, and I choke back a gasp of pain. My immortal body might heal faster than a human's, but it does nothing to mute the sensations. Shade and Tye are wrangling more than a dozen beasts, and Coal is on to killing his fifth. This one bloody sclice is mine.

Letting the beast's momentum carry it by me, I angle my blade to strike the back of its neck. My ribs burn, my pulse racing in fear-tinged fury as I strike.

The sclice twists around, knocking me off my feet. Pouncing on me as I fall, it lands with its clawed front limbs on either side of my head, its oversized lower jaw hanging open, dripping yellow drool onto my neck.

Arching my back, I kick the sclice off, rolling over my shoulder to reclaim my footing. I feel a tiny pulse of satisfaction when none of the males intervenes to rescue me—they're making progress. Then I feel Coal's attention on me, as hot and firm as his hands on my sword arm—all right, slow progress.

Reaching inside myself, I feel for the males' phantom limbs of magic that I'm still getting accustomed to living there. Not one but four cords of power wake to my call, the fledgling magics still developing but eager for freedom. Weaving the four cords into a rough braid, I lash out with a messy weave. So far as we know, I'm the only weaver in all of Lunos—but it will take me centuries to grow into the full breadth of my power.

The braid of magic explodes like the crack of a giant

whip, echoing through the forest. Bits of earth and fern and sclice fly into the air as if caught in some giant shard-filled whirlwind.

"What in the star's name is going on?" River demands, his steady gray eyes taking in the scene while I drop to my knees to catch my breath. "Are you all right, Leralynn?"

I tamp the magic down quickly and back away from the mess. "Yes."

"That's enough for today. Connect," River orders, his crisp words forcing me to my feet. A flash of light has Shade returning to his fae form, black hair swinging over high cheekbones, tan skin, and gleaming yellow eyes. Coal finishes his opponent with an efficient swipe before jogging to where the others are gripping hands.

"Come, lass." Tye extends his hand toward me with a roguish smile and a sparkle in his green eyes, drawing me in to finish the quint's connection. "Playtime's over."

The moment the five of us all touch, the quint's ancient magic fills my body, its thundering power edging out all pain and fatigue. River's competent hands on the magic's reins make short work of pushing the remaining two sclices into the cracked earth before sweeping Coal's kills and my mess into the same abyss and sealing it cleanly.

It's over in seconds, but that rush of joint magic, my heart beating in perfect harmony with four others, brushes my soul with the ecstasy of belonging. *Mine.* No matter their war games, their risk-taking, their maddening overprotectiveness, these males are mine.

2

LERA

I feel no such ecstasy an hour later. Sitting shirtless on Shade's worktable in the Slait Palace, I fidget under four fury-filled glares.

"These cuts are deep, cub," Shade says, his usually velvet voice stern as his fingertips probe my ribs gently. The wolf shifter's magic has a healing affinity, just as Tye's power favors fire and River's speaks with the earth. Coal's odd magic is unique, turned inward on himself after years of slavery, giving him even greater strength, speed, and ability to heal than other fae. Shade crouches for a closer look, his scent of earth fresh from rain filling my nose. Even off the battlefield, Shade moves with lupine grace, his fitted gray pants and bare torso revealing a field of tan, smoothly carved muscles. The beautiful angles of his face are tight with concern. "Had the claws gone a bit farther, you'd have a punctured lung."

9

"I told you to watch your left side, mortal." Coal's blue eyes flash with ice, his tight muscles vibrating with leashed violence. "I didn't know you needed a compass to find 'left.'"

"You needn't have done all that just to win my attention, Lilac Girl." Tye's crossed arms give away the lie behind his voice's lightness. When the male shifts his weight, I see his fists rolled tight enough to bleach the knuckles.

I rub my arms, hoping the feigned chill will conceal the light tremors of fatigued muscles that are now surfacing. "I'm fine."

"And if you weren't, you'd be dead before you admitted it." River steps up beside me, his gray eyes intent on mine. Despite being over five centuries old, the warrior looks to be in his late twenties, his pointed ears and elongated canines as much a marker of his immortality as his aura of power and command. Here in the privacy of Shade's workroom, he's shrugged off his jacket with the king's crest and the small gold crown his subjects expect to see on him, but still, his militantly straight back, close-cropped brown hair, and broad shoulders carry responsibility like a second skin. Even with me sitting on a high table, he towers over me, the largest of the four males, invading my space with a ruthless precision. The weight of his presence—his overwhelming beauty and anger—sends shivers down my skin. "We were out to combine some exercise with utility. There was no cause whatsoever to put yourself in harm's way. If the sclice was giving you trouble, you should have said something. Do you understand me?"

Reaching into myself, I scrape together enough strength to glare right back at River. "You need to give me some space to try out my skills, River. I'm a warrior of the quint now. Would you be fussing if it was Tye sitting here with a few scratches?"

Tye snorts and takes a chair, turning it around to straddle it, eyes on the show.

"We've fought beside Tye over three hundred years. You became fae six months ago." River's voice drops to a low timbre. "More to the point, Tye isn't my mate. For a fae male, the instinct to protect his mate is overwhelming. The moment you became fae and those mating bonds formed, our lives became even more intertwined with yours than they already were. That is something you need to start getting used to, Leralynn. And respecting."

"I've a better idea, River." I straighten my spine, not caring how the movement stings my ribs or pushes my bare chest out farther. "Shade's wolf's instinct is to mark his territory—yet he somehow manages not to piss on the rug. So perhaps your cock could take some instruction from his."

A muscle in River's square jaw tics. Once. Twice. On the third tic, the male turns on his heel and walks out of the room, the door swinging closed behind him. Shade's small, white-walled workroom with its neat, polished surfaces suddenly feels cavernously empty.

When I open my mouth to shout after him, Shade

places his large palm on my cheek, the heat of his body warming the air between us. His yellow eyes are as deep as his voice. "There are very few things in the immortal realm that hurt us more than seeing you in pain, cub." His thumb brushes along my cheekbone the firm pressure sending tendrils of sensation through me. "Protecting you isn't an instinct we *want* to curb."

Strength draining from me, I lean my forehead against Shade's hard chest, the beat of his heart echoing through my skin. "I just want to carry my weight," I whisper, the confession tightening my throat. "Just because magic brought us together—"

"Magic has nothing to do with it." Shade grips my face with both hands, tipping it up to meet his eyes, the fierce possession in them piercing my core. He growls softly, and heat pools in my lower half. "We are your mates, cub. And we would have found you, magic or no, because without you, our souls are incomplete."

Shade leans down until our breaths mix, the heat of his body cocooning my skin. Still holding my face, he presses his mouth against mine, his tongue slipping in gently before claiming me with a predator's possession that reminds me of the wolf he is. The scent of his arousal saturates the air, one hand now sliding down my neck, my shoulder, my collarbone. Cupping my right breast.

My skin tingles beneath the male's touch, the breast in his hold suddenly full and aching. My insides tighten, as much from the thoroughly claiming kiss as at the thought of Shade's mouth elsewhere. Suckling the sensitive breast he now holds. Dipping lower.

Shade's callused thumb brushes against my nipple, a shudder running though his body when the bud peaks in response. Molten heat flows down my core, my sex, the backs of my thighs, making even my toes tingle with need.

I'll never get used to this. No matter how many times we drown in the mating bond, on how many surfaces in how many palace rooms and quiet passages and curtained nooks we give in to lust, casual talking turning to breathless claiming. I only seem to want them more with each passing day.

"If I knew we were bypassing the healing and scolding and moving right to kissing, I'd have moved closer," says Tye. His deep, amused voice only heightens the ache in my sex, as images of what the three of us could do together right now flood my imagination—the four of us, if Coal would just stop sharpening that damn knife.

Shade chuckles against my mouth, pressing into me until I feel the hardness pulsating inside his breeches. I slide my hand to grip his taut backside, pulling him even closer—

"You need to finish up in here." River's voice cuts between us, the air chilling with the open door. For a moment, I think the male has returned to argue some more, and the frustration gripping my sex mixes violently with the retort bubbling inside my chest. But then I hear it. An uncharacteristic tightness in River's tone—a barely reined-in tension that makes my stomach clench. Shade

13

straightens, giving my thigh an apologetic squeeze, and I slide to my feet.

"What's happened?" Coming up behind me, Tye wraps his jacket around me, his heavy hand staying comfortingly on my shoulder as his eyes watch River's every move.

River runs his hand through his short hair, his one tell surfacing. "A message from the Elders Council," he says quietly. "The wards protecting the mortal realm from magic have cracked."

3

LERA

*W*ith Shade's healing magic still tingling along my skin, I let myself into what was once a formal sitting room for River's father, Griorgi, but which now resembles a cross of den and library. Tall windows flood the chamber with brilliant sunlight, illuminating the colorful frescos of fae history covering each wall. Griorgi's high-backed carved wooden chairs have been evicted in favor of more comfortable leather furniture, and a smell of sweet wine and bitter chocolate announces that both Tye and Autumn, River's brilliant sister, have already made themselves comfortable.

"The wards protecting the mortal realm from magic have cracked." River's words echo in my mind, twisting and turning in search of some plausible explanation. A millennium ago, after the fae and humans enslaved in the

dark realm of Mors broke free, the most powerful of the immortals combined their magics to separate the world into three realms. The dark realm of Mors, where the terrifying gray-skinned qoru rule. The immortal realm of Lunos for the fae. And the largest, the mortal realm, where all the human kingdoms find a home.

Last year, Griorgi attempted an alliance with the Mors emperor, opening a portal between Lunos and Mors. That escapade nearly destroyed Blaze, one of Lunos's three courts. A penetration into the mortal realm, whose denizens have little to no knowledge of fae and no way to defend themselves, would be infinitely more deadly.

"Lera!" Autumn looks up from a sea of reference books, her many silver-blond braids swaying. Her fashion, as usual, puts my simple black fighting leathers to shame— a flowing dress of green and turquoise silk belted tight around her tiny waist. The sparkling silver at her ears, wrists, and neck make her look like every inch the princess she is, though it is the small leather cap sitting atop her left ear that the female fingers most often—a gift from her lover, Kora. "River said you are hurt."

I throw River a dagger-filled look. "I thought River wanted to talk about broken wards, not keep worrying over three scratches."

River lifts one brow, his gray eyes unreadable. "I can worry and talk simultaneously."

"Forget I asked," Autumn says quickly, tossing me a quick, conspiratorial smile before turning back to her books.

"Did Mystwood burn down?" I ask, setting a course for my favorite armchair. A shiver runs through me at the thought of the deep, mystical forest separating Lunos from the mortal realm. A forest I used to live at the edge of. It was created to prevent fae—and other, much darker immortal creatures—from walking into mortal lands, a fact my males were able to circumvent to come find me only by way of a highly rare and powerful passage key.

"Mystwood still stands," says River, stepping aside as Shade's wolf streaks across the room.

"Don't you dare," I yell after the beast, who is already leaping from the floor.

Too late. With a self-satisfied snort, Shade lands lightly on my chair and circles in place several times before curling into a large gray ball—one paw, tail, and tongue strategically extended to claim the entire seat.

One yellow eye blinks back at me piously.

I glower at him. "Get off, or I'll sit on you."

"That is not much of a disincentive, Lilac Girl," says Tye, pulling me into his own lap as he settles on the couch. The male's powerful thigh muscles shift to brace my backside, his white-silk-covered arms and scent of pine and citrus flowing like water around me. When I squirm to get free, a set of tiny, very dangerously placed sparks of fire magic nip me beneath my tight leather pants.

I gasp, and Tye clicks his tongue right next to my ear. "You really should stay put, lass. For safety's sake and all that."

"Enough," River says from the middle of the room, his

hands laced at the small of his back. With a jerk of his chin, the male nods to the low table where a map and stack of papers are already spread. Scout reports, by the look of them. A great many reports. "While we were out playing with sclices, the Elders Council delivered disturbing news. While Mystwood is intact, there is a weakness in the fabric separating the mortal realms of Light and Gloom. Creatures such as sclices have been spotted in the human world, and our fae scouts have even felt traces of their own magic when the mortal realm should have shackled their power completely. If left unaddressed this one point of weakness will spiderweb out like a crack in a glass."

"I don't understand how that's possible if Mystwood stands," I say.

"Mystwood forest is a wall," says Autumn, rising and pushing River lightly to the side to stand before us. She holds one hand perpendicular to the other palm, her gray eyes blazing with the results of her research. "This wall stops magic and forbids traffic between Lunos and the human world, but it doesn't extend infinitely. Go deep enough into the Gloom and you can get under the wall— but since you can't *exit* the Gloom on the mortal side, this has never mattered."

"Until now," I finish for her.

"Yes," Autumn says. "Since Mystwood is intact, yet traces of magic and Mors vermin have appeared in the human world, we believe there is a rip in the fabric.

Fortunately, all the anomalies are centered around a single location. For now. As River stated, if left unchecked, the rip will spread and the impact will become catastrophic."

"The territory with the anomalies belongs to Great Falls Academy, in the mortal realm." Taking over for his sister, River steps toward the table and traces an area on the map, his callused finger circling what looks like a small town surrounded by a great stretch of forested wilderness. "Have you heard of it, Leralynn?"

I wince. Even during my isolated life tending horses at Zake's estate, I'd heard of the place—its reputation precedes it. And then some. "Great Falls is the most prestigious school on the continent, catering to royals and nobles of all ten kingdoms in the Continental Alliance. The king of Ckridel set it up two hundred years ago when the alliance was first formed, following the theory that if you sequester the ten kingdoms' future leaders into joint, high-quality misery for a few years, they'll emerge not only well trained but with an aversion to slaughtering each other in the future. And it's worked."

"Not a bad notion." River runs his hand through his hair. "But rather inconvenient at the moment, as that's the only real place from which to launch a reconnaissance mission."

"I presume the Elders Council wants us to go find out the size and cause of this crack and fix it before the sclices eat the Alliance's future rulers for supper?" says Coal, though we all know the rodents would be the least of the humans' problems if a full passage between the Light and Gloom opened up. Not everyone's ancestors were fortunate enough to escape the qoru, and Coal still wakes with nightmares of his time there as a slave. Emperor Jawrar would jump at another chance to find a foothold beyond Mors's borders, a thought that sends cold dread spiraling through me.

"Yes." River sighs. "With Leralynn being from the mortal lands, and considering the strength of our quint, the Elders believe us uniquely suited for the mission. While my being Slait's ruler on my own court's territory prevents the Council from *ordering* us to go, they are asking us to."

Placing the fate of thousands of lives on our—on *River's*—unerringly responsible shoulders.

The room falls silent, tension in every breath.

The Council doesn't make a habit of requesting anything. That they are doing so now—instead of waiting until River stepped off Slait soil and thus into the Council's jurisdiction—means the situation is dire indeed. There are few quints in Lunos who match the males' experience and skill, and none but the Council itself who rival our joint power.

"They are right," I say, watching River's face tighten even as his hand twitches toward the map. He wants to go. They all do. The six months of staying put since River took the throne is driving the males stir-crazy—their frustration matched only by their bullheaded overprotectiveness. "How would we get into the Academy, though?" I ask, strategically turning the discussion away from *whether* we should be going. "Human legends peg fae for murderous monsters. Anyone in charge of an academy filled with the sons and daughters of the kingdoms' most influential families would order the lot of us killed on sight."

"That problem I can solve." Autumn leans forward, the sparkle in her eyes saying she's been mulling the puzzle over for some time. "You'll get in wearing chameleon veils. Warded amulets that alter the beholder's perception of who you are and why you are there."

"Wait." I hold up my hand. "I thought magic doesn't work in the mortal realm."

"True. With the exception of passive magic, such as our immortality, the mortal realm does shackle all outward power—Tye's fire affinity, Shade's healing, River's earth will all be unusable," says Autumn. "Shifting is all but impossible, and don't ask me about Coal's magic, because the stars only know what that does. But *physical* wards—those attached to objects like this amulet—tend to still function if they are powerful enough."

Opening a wooden box that I hadn't noticed in her lap, the female removes a set of five intricately carved wooden amulets. They're nearly identical circular medallions with a delicate lacelike pattern spreading out in points from the center. "And these are some of the most complex and powerful magics in Lunos. They go beyond the basics and truly build a whole history for each of you, depending on where you are in the mortal world."

"So if Tye were to put a veil on and step into a monastery—" River starts to say.

"—the monastery residents would see him as an acolyte or a fellow monk," Autumn finishes for him. "Possibly as one who's been there for some time. Moreover, the amulet would use facts from Tye's actual history to build the new legend. So with Tye being a high-level flex athlete, his legend would likely include an explanation for athletic prowess."

"Why would the veil make him appear a monk and not a chamber-pot boy?" asks Coal, earning a dirty look from Tye. "That would fit too."

Autumn shrugs one smooth, bare shoulder. "The veil could very well make him a chamber-pot boy, especially if this monastery made a habit of hiring former athletes to clean rooms—the magic follows the path of least resistance. That is the first limitation of the veil amulets: you've no control over the legend they spin for you, and once the legend is created, it doesn't alter. The amulet is designed to convince the world you belong there—it little cares whether you find the role convenient. For this reason, I'd advise never to wear a new veil into a prison, lest it convinces the guards you belong there as an inmate."

"How will we know what legend the veil created for us?" I ask.

"The amulet will give you an awareness of it, a phantom desire to believe that it is true. This brings me to the veil's second limitation—you must remove the amulet for at least an hour each day, lest you fall victim to the veil yourself."

"Any other limitations?" River asks, picking up one of the amulets and twisting it suspiciously in his fingers.

"One more." Autumn bites her lip, her voice apologetic. "The amulets' magic builds a disguise so complete that it mutes all bonds. You will feel neither the quint nor your mating bond while you wear them."

4

LERA

"I don't think we should go," River says, letting himself into my bedchamber a few hours after our briefing. Closing the door with a soft click, he strides to where I'm already packing, my clothes and weapons laid out neatly atop the four-poster bed. "I can't leave the throne only six months after taking it."

My jaw tightens at both the lie and the reason behind it. "I imagine Autumn can manage the day-to-day operation. Given the few centuries of experience she has at it." Three centuries, to be exact—all the time River stayed away from Slait Court, returning only six months ago to finally depose the monster who sat on the throne.

River has the decency to blush.

I cross my arms, glaring up at him—not an easy feat with how close the large male is standing to me. With his straight back and broad shoulders, corded thighs and mirror-shined black boots spread slightly apart for balance, River eclipses the world without trying. But he isn't going to eclipse me. "If you've come to tell me how much your male instincts will hurt if I—"

"But you *died* six months ago," River snaps, the sudden break of his iron control vibrating the room. His shadowed gray eyes study me with such intensity that my chest tightens. He swallows, a slight tremor running through him. "I still feel the terror of that moment every time I close my eyes. So yes, Leralynn, I hate seeing you in danger. In pain. There is nothing in Lunos or the mortal lands that's worth that for me. For any of us four. Someone else can go."

"Stars. River." The anger simmering my blood softens, and I reach up to trace my fingers along the angle of his square jaw. The tension inside him radiates through the skin, the muscles shifting beneath my fingers. The rare glimpse into my quint commander's vulnerability makes my stomach clench. But it doesn't change reality. "Then I think it's fortunate for both realms that at least one of us can think clearly," I say gently.

"Leralynn." River's voice drops, his hands gripping my hips.

I shake my head. "Someone else didn't grow up in the mortal realm. Someone else isn't a weaver. And someone else is certainly not part of the second most powerful quint in all of Lunos. We might be mated, but we are still a warrior quint. We were chosen by the magic to go out and *do* things. And this is the first of many."

River closes his eyes, his chest expanding with his breaths. A heartbeat later, he pulls me fiercely against him. "Two points of clarification," he whispers, his warm breath ruffling the hair on the top of my head. "First, once we discover the full extent of your new weaving magic, we might be *the* most powerful. And second... No matter how powerful you may one day become, I will always want to keep you safe. It is a hazard you'll be forced to weather for centuries, Leralynn."

"You are blaming the mating bond for making you insufferable?" I swallow, sounding hoarse as that very bond rouses to River's woodsy scent and caresses my soul. "Seems rather convenient."

Taking my chin between his thumb and forefinger, River raises my gaze toward him. His gray eyes study me, shifting into commanding intimacy. "Very convenient," he echoes, his strong face filling my vision, his shoulders blocking the world from view. A purposeful motion, and one that makes my heart stutter in spite of itself.

River's singular undiluted attention fills me, holding me in place as heat floods my sex. My hand twitches toward him, and he stills my motion with a look, my thighs clenching together in a mix of need and outrage.

A pleased, knowing glint fills River's gray eyes, his nostrils flaring delicately. "Yes, I smell it," he whispers into my ear, his gaze trailing down my abdomen until there is no question as to what precisely he refers to.

Heat touches my cheeks.

"You are beautiful when you blush," River whispers. This close, I can feel the pounding of his heart, striking his ribs as hard as my own. His free hand slides down the curve of my hip and thigh, lifting the silk hem of my lavender nightgown. Cool air brushes my thighs a moment before River's warm hand trails up the sensitive skin, dipping unapologetically inside my undergarments toward the dampness I know is there.

Stars. Even after six months, the intensity of my new fae body still comes as a shock. It isn't just the longer, shinier hair and smoother, near-glowing skin, it's the avalanche of sensation. What used to merely arouse me now drives me insane with want.

I squirm on instinct, and River's other hand drops from my face to cup my backside firmly, keeping me in place as he slides through my slickness. Extracting his glistening hand, he licks his fingers clean, growling with soft pleasure.

Stars. I open my mouth to—

River's lips capture mine, swallowing whatever protest I was about to utter.

My body tenses, River's claiming flooding me with sensation so intense, I can't stay still. Yet I can't move either. Not with the male's hands and mouth on me, his feet shifting to trap mine between them. Giving me no escape. No chance to do anything but feel him. Feel us.

One heartbeat builds on the next until the slow

throbbing vibrating through my core grows so insistent, I am gasping for air. Pulling back slightly, River scrapes the points of elongated canines along my bottom lip, making me writhe beneath his hands despite certain consequences.

River chuckles, his hand slipping right back beneath my skirt, up my damn inner thigh and—I gasp as a finger slides inside me, his thumb flicking over the sensitive apex. A zing spiders along my skin, my sex clenching around the glorious intrusion, the burst of sensation both too much and not nearly enough. When the callused tip of River's finger traces my hood, I whimper outright, rising onto my toes for relief that won't come.

River's lips brush my ear. "I can ignore the mating bond's instinct no more than you can ignore this, luv." Another trace along my hood, coupled with tiny flicks on either side of my apex until I'm squirming despite his hold. "But please, try as hard as you like."

"Bastard." Raising my hands, I rake them over River's back, the press of his hardness against my mound dizzyingly satisfying.

With a growl, he pushes me away to arm's length, his breaths ragged, his gray eyes gleaming with barely restrained need. A predator targeting prey. With the next breath, River shoves me back and back, until my thighs press against the edge of my bed and my breaths come in ragged, desperate gasps. With a sweep of one thickly muscled arm, my neat piles are strewn across the floor.

"Those are my travel clothes," I warn.

"I'll get you new ones." The sound of ripping silk swallows River's words, the room's cool air brushing my exposed skin for a moment before his muscular body settles atop mine.

River frees himself in one practiced movement, the thick head of his engorged cock coating itself in my wetness. Even after all these months, the size of him sends ripples of warning through my body, my channel already tasting the stretch—the fullness—to come. Gripping my thighs in an undeniable hold, River finds my eyes as he positions himself at my entrance, his eyes shining with desire and conquest. Savoring my anxious anticipation, the bastard.

"I'll murder you in your sleep," I warn through clenched teeth, my empty, empty sex clenching around nothingness while the thoroughly aroused apex sends zinging pulses down to my toes.

River's teeth flash, the power of him suddenly filling every inch of air in the room. Five centuries of battle-honed muscles, of leading the realm's greatest warriors, all flash in reminder of who exactly stands between my open thighs. "Just for that..." The warning in River's voice shoots through me a moment before he lowers his mouth right atop my bud and *sucks*.

My whole body tightens, the pleasure mounting so fast and hard that it turns to liquid agony and back, a bow stretching further and further and—

River stops.

No. No. No. My body trembles in anticipation, in the all-consuming need to release that tautly pulled bow. I buck desperately, come up against River's unyielding hold, and finally whimper.

With a pleased chuckle, River sheathes himself inside me, his thickness everything I wanted and feared. In and back, in and back, the powerful *thrust thrust thrust* of his cock gathers all the needy nerves inside me. My heart quickens, my breath coming in little pants while my eyes see nothing but the strong line of River's jaw and the flex of corded muscle beneath his well-cut tunic.

Thrust thrust thrust.

River's shaft pulses, my channel clenching around it. Every fiber in my lower body screams, feeling the approaching abyss. This time, my wild, needy, desperate bucking is beyond my control. But not beyond River's, who holds my thighs with unyielding command.

Thrust, thrust...

The explosion of pleasure rakes through my body, lighting every nerve. Anguish so fierce, it is pure bliss. My muscles tighten, my sex clenches, my vision blurs. Tumbling into the great abyss inside me, I feel River's own release filling my channel and realize the warrior is trembling as badly as I am.

THERE ARE FOUR WRAPPED BUNDLES, in addition to

Autumn, Kora, and the males, waiting for me in the stables the following morning. Settling my saddlebags beside Sprite, the dapple-gray mare River gifted me with when I first came to Lunos, I study the gathering suspiciously. "What's happening?"

"We—" Autumn starts, then rolls her eyes at the males and picks up one of the larger bundles, thrusting it into my arms. "*I* thought that your first official mission as a quint warrior was worth celebrating. So, here. This is from me."

"Wasn't dethroning King Griorgi the first?" I ask.

"No. That was housekeeping." Autumn nods at the package that I unwrap to reveal a gown of soft red silk, a matching shawl completing the look. "Dress in this before you put on the veil and enter the Academy, all right?" She pulls her own shimmering silver wrap more tightly around her slender shoulders and looks down, suddenly finding its woven edge endlessly fascinating. Her eyes glisten slightly in the morning sun. "The veil can't make you a chamber-pot girl in that. At least I don't think it can. I—"

I throw my arms around my friend, who hugs me back fiercely, letting go only when Kora puts a comforting arm on Autumn's shoulder, drawing her lover away.

"Thank you." I kiss Autumn's cheek before looking up at her brother, who holds his package with uncharacteristic hesitation. Taking River's gift, I unwrap the paper gingerly and feel my chest tighten at the intricate handiwork. Four cords in different sparkling shades of gold woven together into a braid, the pendent hanging from them a complex knot of the same strands. I look closer and gasp in recognition. One strand is studded with amethysts—Coal's strange purple magic; one with deep brown-red garnets—River's earth magic; one with yellow-orange diamonds—Tye's fire; and one with gleaming silver—Shade's healing. "The cords of your four magics plaited together with my weaver's gift," I whisper, running my fingers over the priceless piece. "This must have taken the jeweler months."

River shrugs one massive shoulder, but there is a bit of color in his cheeks when I turn to let him fasten the treasure around my neck.

Shade steps up next, his package holding a pair of gray mittens. Inhaling the wool's familiar earthy scent, I narrow my eyes at the shifter. "Where exactly did you get these?"

A flash of light has a wolf replacing the male, the animal's long tongue licking the tip of his nose virtuously. Now that I'm paying closer attention, I see the wolf's shortened coat and wince. "How many weavers did you bite in the making of these mittens?" I ask.

"Four," Autumn informs me dryly. "Two of them submitted resignations."

The wolf, suddenly finding a tree in need of careful sniffing, trots off while Tye hands me the heaviest package yet. Instead of paper, this one is wrapped in sturdy cloth, rolled up tightly and buckled closed. He winks as I take it, making my heart beat faster. He's ridiculously handsome in his fitted leather riding pants and billowing white shirt, opened at the collar to reveal the muscled flare of his pectorals. And he knows it. I roll my eyes, making him grin wider.

Laying the bundle on a nearby tree stump, I unroll it carefully and stare at the thin polished instruments. No. No, it can't be. "Are these…"

"Lockpicks," Tye supplies helpfully. "Aye."

River curses.

"These are…" I struggle to find the right word. "Gorgeous" doesn't seem to fit the objects and "a sure way to get arrested" doesn't fit the mood. "High-quality tools of a trade I don't quite know."

Tye sighs gravely. "I was afraid of that. I will have to teach you, then, lass." His emerald eyes sparkle. "Though I must warn you, I'm a very hands-on type of instructor."

I snap the kit closed very quickly, then stuff it into my saddlebag. When I step away, I find Coal's blue eyes watching me from the side. Five fae and four packages. Coal isn't the type for sentimentality. I nod my understanding at him.

Coal turns away.

A heartbeat later, a glistening boot dagger whizzes so close to my ear that I hear the whistle of air as it flies by. With a dull thump, the blade impales itself into a tree, the hilt still vibrating from the impact. Saying nothing, Coal mounts his horse, leaving me to collect my final gift in silence.

With everyone mounted up, River lays a large hand on his sister's shoulders, Autumn reaching up to grasp his muscled forearm. The siblings trade no words, and I wonder how many such goodbyes they've exchanged over the centuries—each time knowing they might not be quite the same beings when they meet next. Before I can dwell on the thought, River clicks to his stallion and leads us to Great Falls Academy.

5

LERA

*T*he ride to Mystwood's edge is quiet and efficient. Letting the horses rest and water before we enter the warded forest, River pulls out a saucer-sized disk carved with runes—one of the few keys permitting the bearers passage through the forest. The magic radiating from the relic tickles my skin, drawing me toward it.

"Stay together. We've a small radius," River says, his calm voice a beacon as I ready to step into the Gloom— one of the new and rare skills my fae body came equipped with. Which makes entering it no more pleasant than it was when the males had to tow me along.

The air around me thickens, a moment of viscous blackness pushing against me on all sides, and then I'm in the dull echo of the world. The colors and noises and smells are all short of what they should be—shades of gray and strange echoes. Wrong. But travel is faster here—and when it comes to Mystwood, traveling through the Gloom is the only way possible to traverse the place. Even with the key.

River once explained the Gloom as an underlining to the normal world—what we call the Light—a slippery undercloth that shifts and moves with the main cloth but is separate from it as well. Some of the stitching, like many of Mystwood's ash and maple trees, penetrate all the way through. Other pieces, like much of the shrubbery, exist only in the Light. Poetic, but I've worked out my own, more practical, definition.

The Gloom is where creatures of darkness and evil thrive and roam, unseen in the Light until they are ready to rise and strike. Something that can never be permitted to happen in the mortal realm.

This is my second time crossing Mystwood, the first being when the males whisked me away from servitude in Zake's stable. Now, returning as a fae warrior myself, I expect the forest to seem less oppressive. In reality, the opposite is true.

"One nice thing about being human is that you don't know what goes bump in the shadows, Lilac Girl," Tye says, stretching lazily beside me—seeming to read my mind as usual. "Which is why I make it a personal goal to know as little as possible about everything."

We move along with little conversation, Shade's wolf keeping as close to us as the horses will tolerate. When the five of us clear Mystwood less than six hours later, stepping into the Light just before the edge of the mortal realm, the muted oppression of the Gloom finally melts away—only to reveal a new set of shackles one step later. My magic. Lashed down as tightly as a ship's furled sails.

Having lived most of my life without the magic, I thought this part would little bother me, but the emptiness grips my throat. Looking around with my immortal's heightened senses, I mourn the loss of Lunos's lush intensity even as I pick up each sound and smell the way my human body never could.

With so few humans willing to live anywhere near the edge of Mystwood, it's relatively easy to keep out of the humans' sight during the four-day ride to the town of Great Falls, which takes its name from a tall, narrow waterfall rushing over a cliff high in the mountains on the right. Its roar echoes distantly around the small, steep valley, over the patchwork sheep meadows and neat timber-frame houses. The lonely screech of circling ravens and a stiff breeze mark our passage across a bare, grassy ridge above the valley.

Stopping at an overlook a mile off, I raise my hand to block out the sun as I examine the Academy's estate sprawling at the top of a foothill overlooking the town. An immense walled-off fortress of gray stone, blending into the mountains behind it, its gilded red standard flapping on the cold wind. The hiss and crack of the fabric cuts into my hearing. I frown. Even with my fae senses, the flapping cloth is too far away to be heard. No, the hiss and crack is coming from something else, though it certainly sounds like a flapping flag.

I glance around, Sprite dancing beneath me enough to earn a disapproving glance from Coal. Nothing about him or the other males suggests they hear anything amiss. In fact—I realize with a start—River is speaking.

"...A generation of influential youth all in one place." The quint commander pats his stallion's neck, his voice filled with a responsibility he can't help. Perhaps that need to take charge is what makes River who he is. "I hope the staff have a firm bit in the youngsters' mouths before the would-be kings decide to compare the size of their cocks and do something unusually stupid."

Hiss crack crack.

My pulse jumps.

"Lass?" Tye frowns. "Are you—"

"They aren't children," I say quickly, forcing my voice into mild outrage to knock Tye's inconvenient perceptiveness off scent. After all my insistence over us coming here, at the first sight of our battleground, I'm already hearing phantom noises. "Twenty years might be nothing for fae, but for a human, it's rather significant. It also happens to be my age."

"My point exactly," says River. "Let's get this done. Remember what Autumn said about muted bonds and brace yourselves for the change." Taking out the veil amulet, the male snaps it around his neck with no ceremony, the others wordlessly following his example. The intricately carved wood medallions fall against their sternums until they each tuck them away under their shirts.

Hiss crack crack.

I fumble for my own amulet, a chill running over my skin as I settle it around my neck. The soft click of the clasp is one of the loudest sounds I've ever heard—a slamming door cutting me off from the males. My lungs tighten painfully, and it takes all my willpower to keep my hands light on Sprite's reins. To raise my chin. To smile with a cockiness I wish I felt.

"So, then," I say, realizing too late that I've forgotten to don the dress Autumn gave me. Damn it. I'll do it as soon as we find a less exposed spot on our way to the Academy. In my black pants and favorite fitted blue tunic, belted around the waist, the magic could give me a disguise for just about anyone. "What am I now?"

"A pain in the ass," says Coal, the carved angles of his face still as he cocks a brow at me.

"We know you, cub. The amulet won't spin a veil for those who know the truth," Shade, now in his fae form, says gently. "We look like ourselves to you too, do we not?"

"Right. Of course." I rub my eyes with the heel of my hand.

"What's wrong, Lilac Girl?" Tye asks.

"Nothing. I mean I can't feel you with the amulet. And—"

Tye winces. "It does hurt me to see you lie so poorly, lass. We need to work on that. What is it?"

I sigh, shaking my head. "Just an odd noise I heard. A

hissing sound, like…static, but louder. Do you hear it?"

They pause, cocking their heads in concentration.

"No," says Tye after a moment, Shade, Coal, and River echo their agreement, their eyes kind—and somewhat worried.

Heat fills my cheeks, but River raises his hand, stopping my attempt to apologize. "Us not hearing it doesn't mean nothing is there. Your magic is unique, Leralynn. A human made fae, a weaver to boot. It is entirely possible you are hearing escaping magic. Perhaps the very rift we are here to find."

"Or my own imagination."

River shrugs one shoulder. "Indeed. But, being immortal we've the time to check. Where is the sound coming from?"

"It's…" The words die in my mouth. Nothing. I hear nothing now but my own racing heart. The heat already touching my cheeks spreads to make the tips of my ears tingle. Swallowing, I close my eyes, willing myself to find the sound again. Nothing. "May I take the amulet off? Perhaps it's interfering with the sound."

River's gaze weighs the distance to the Academy before he nods. "For a bit."

I open the clasp and shove the amulet into my breast pocket, relief flooding me as the mating bonds call to me once more—and the static. At least I wasn't imagining the noise. "This way." Nudging Sprite into a trot, I lead the males toward the sound, which grows louder with each step. Overwhelming. We cross into a whispering green aspen wood, light flickering through the leaves in dizzying patterns. My muscles tense, my breath and heart speeding as Sprite picks up a gallop along a narrow uphill trail. The hooves of the males' stallions keep pace, staying far enough back to avoid sending the horses into a competitive race, which would likely end with me on the ground.

Hiss crack crack. Hiss crack crack.

The trail swings sharply to the right, but with sound coming so clearly from behind a cluster of huge boulders on the opposite side, I nudge my mount that way. Sprite takes the left at alarming speed, her body angling sharply. I have no time to twist around and make sure the males saw me turn off the trail, no ability to do anything but cling on with every muscle fiber. Sprite's hooves pound the uneven ground, the horse out of control as she races for the boulders, which prove farther away than I'd guessed. Branches whip, clumps of earth flying into the air. I grab the pommel of my saddle to keep my seat, the reins loosening in my hands. My legs squeeze the horse's sides, my instinctual clinging unfortunately signaling Sprite to run faster still.

HISS. CRACK—

I see the crumbling rune-carved stone embedded in the ground a heartbeat before Sprite trips over it. The tenuous hold I have on my saddle breaks, sending me to the ground. My head cracks against a rock, the sound coming before the pain. Then the world flashes in a blaze of blinding light before darkness comes.

6

LERA

J wake with a horse's nose poking my back, the clicking aspen forest sprawling its spring glory before me. My head hurts, but I find no blood when I touch my skull. Small miracle. I also find no one else beside me.

"River?" I call, my pulse hammering. "Coal? Tye? Shade?"

Silence. A few paces away, the rune-carved stone Sprite tripped over is broken into hand-sized bits. By the looks of it, the thing was a square slate about the length of a man's forearm on each side and pushed into the cold earth like a misaligned paving stone. The noise from it—if there ever was a noise—is gone. Picking up one of the shards, I realize the thing wasn't stone all the way through, but rather just a hard shell protecting a softer claylike core that leaves dust on my fingers.

"River?" I call again. "Anyone?"

Only chattering birds answer, and the ghostly whispering of bright-green leaves.

Sprite whinnies, stomping one foot with a loose shoe. Damn it. Bending down, I pull the shoe the rest of the way off and toss it away. I'll be walking the horse from here on out. But walking her to where?

Holding Sprite by her reins, I slowly retrace the path we galloped, through slants of golden evening light. The tracks curve downhill, turning sharply toward the narrow trail Sprite and I had run. Here, several sets of diverging hoofprints lead in all directions. As if some riders had followed the trail to the right—where I'd gone left—and others turned their horses around completely, heading back to a wider road. Or perhaps the mounts had spooked and run.

I shake my head, instantly regretting the motion as pain slices down the back of my skull. *Think, Lera. What exactly happened?* Forcing my breathing to steady, I think back. I recall cantering. No, galloping. The males giving me space, but not staying far back. Then the trail went right. But I didn't. I turned off the trail and headed sharply left. Sprite broke into a gallop over bad terrain. She tripped. I fell, hitting my head. Losing consciousness. With the thick green foliage and sharp turn, the males might not have seen me take the turn and fall, but surely they should have found me by now.

Except they didn't.

By the looks of the horse tracks, they went the other

way entirely. I sigh, pulling myself together. I've no notion how long I was unconscious, but from the sun's movement, it was some time. Whatever the reason the males left, they are now either too far to hear me yell or not in a position to answer. Perhaps, with the mating bond muted by their amulets, they don't feel me—or their fear for me—as fiercely as they normally would. I don't feel them at all, though my fear is perfectly intact. The reality of existence without the bond's pull sends a chill down my spine, despite knowing it would happen. Bracing a hand against a tree, I take a deep breath and force my mind to function. Plan. I've two choices now by my reckoning: either stay here in the middle of the woods, hoping to be rescued before the predators decide I'm dinner, or continue to the Academy as planned and work things through there.

My hands tremble as I take up Sprite's reins, leading the mare down the path. I slip on my veil amulet lest I cross paths with anyone, shivering at the feelings that pass over me—the deadening of deafened mating bonds, the faint vertigo that comes from pulling an alternate identity over me like a cloak.

To my relief, the amulet remained intact during the fall, along with my saddlebags. I try to focus on that. On anything except why no one is here. There is an explanation for this. There has to be. This is but a hiccup, I promise myself, refusing to let the thickening woods and lengthening shadows, the rising hoot of an owl, the crunching step of an unseen animal, close around me.

With the Academy clearly visible atop high ground, I

keep my course set on its flapping standard. Winding trails come and go along steep hills, but I keep straight and move quickly, talking to Sprite softly as we walk unwaveringly between trees. "We are Sprite and Lera," I tell Sprite, who nickers in agreement. "I am a fae female of a warrior quint. And we are here to discover what's letting magic leak into the human world. We are here to save people. We aren't afraid."

It's well past sunset by the time Sprite and I finally make it to the Academy wall, dark-gray stone rising into the blackness above me, topped with flickering torches. A heavy wooden gate with iron spikes the width of my thigh rises on creaking pulleys to let me into a vestibule, the secondary gate remaining closed.

The uniformed guard who let me in frowns, lowering the spiked gate back down behind Sprite and me. Trapping us between the two exits. "It is past curfew," he says, his black brows narrowing. He's the first human I've seen up close in months, and I instantly notice the differences—the blunter features, as if seen through a foggy lens, the shorter stature and softer frame.

I lick my dry lips. "I'm..." The amulet warms against my sternum, phantom memories shimmering in my mind, changing my history.

The estate that I grew up in as Zake's indentured servant becomes a mansion with high vaulted ceilings and plush rugs. My old clothes shift from a stable hand's ill-fitting rags to a too-tight tailored dress embroidered with a coat of arms. The belt that beat me raw still remains in my memories, though the lord wielding it now presses me against an upholstered wall instead of a stable's rough wood for the lashings.

I'm a noble-born orphan, my new memories tell me. Taken in by Lord Zake of Osprey and raised as his ward. I have no friends.

I clear my throat and try again. "I'm—"

"Leralynn of Osprey," the guard finishes for me. "I'm aware of who you are. But not why you are late. Great Falls Academy, you will discover, does not tolerate tardiness. Nor do we tolerate students roaming the wilderness. In fact, Commander River—that's the Academy's deputy headmaster who took up the late Commander Jun's vacant post five months ago—has ordered that anyone found in violation of curfew be sent directly to him."

"River?" My breath catches, relief and anxiety filling my chest. The amulets are working, and my males—at least one of them—is here. It's all right. Whatever the reason River never circled back to get me, I'll discover it shortly. I am not alone. "River is here?" I repeat, not realizing I've grabbed the guard's wrist until he cocks a thick brow at me.

"Take a breath, girl." The man softens his voice, apparently taking my behavior as a sign that the appropriate level of terror has been instilled. "I won't report you, just this once. Though if I were you, I'd endeavor to know as little of the captain as you do now." He motions for the inner doors to be opened and leads me into the Academy's sleeping campus, while one of the other guards takes charge of Sprite.

A quick mental analysis confirms I have no choice but to follow him, to play along with my disguise until I can gather more information. No matter how much I long to run through the Academy shouting River's name, I'm here for a mission—one that I can't risk because I'm too frightened to spend a night alone. Plus, the danger of being discovered as fae in these parts is not lost on me either—I little need a farmer or hunter trying to plant an axe between my shoulder blades. Avoiding the desire to finger my amulet, I follow the guard meekly.

Even in the night's darkness, my immortal eyes mark the Academy's grand sprawl. Stone buildings rising several stories into the air on all sides of us, the distant neigh of stabled horses, cobblestone passages, and quietly burbling fountains.

"The physical training and maneuvers take place in the yard on the east side of the Academy." The guard points as we walk across the broad central square, our footsteps echoing hollowly in the silence. "The dormitories are in the southwest. Academic lessons take place in the keep, to the northwest." It's obvious which building he means—an immense castle with pointed spires blocking the stars directly behind us. The fortress on the hill that can be seen for miles, its flapping red standard my earlier guide.

Leading me into a square building with a small stone

courtyard in its center, the guard takes the external whitewashed walkways to bring me up to the second story.

"Bedchamber 241," the guard says, unaware that my fae eyes let me read the lettering for myself. He hands me a key. "You share it with Arisha of Tallie. Tomorrow, you may collect your issued supplies and your allowance from the quartermaster. Most of our new students find the adjustment to the Academy's discipline difficult. For your sake, I suggest you adapt quickly. Treat the guards and instructors with the reverence you would offer your elders at home, and you will do well. You may be my superior in a ballroom, but here, at Great Falls, you are a student."

The last is said with no malice, and I thank the male— the man—demurely before ducking into the darkened room, a girl's soft snores the only sound to counter my pounding head. River, at least, has made it. As the bloody deputy headmaster. I rub my temple. It does fit, given his overprotective and in-constant-charge personality. The others I'll have to find in the morning. Along with the reason they all left me behind.

7

LERA

"*L*eralynn, wake up." A female voice urges me from sleep.

Blinking my eyes open, I find myself staring at a comely girl about my age, with frizzy brown hair and large eyes. For a few seconds, all I can do is stare at her rounded ear tips. *Arisha of Tallie,* my memory of the guard's words last night tells me. My roommate. I lift my still-aching head, the warming amulet reminding me that I'm a new student. A lady. Leralynn of Osprey, sent here to study with other prominent youths. For a moment, the story is so persuasive that my heart skips a beat as I scramble out of bed. I was late coming in last night, and if I am late again this morning—

Lera. I am Leralynn, a warrior of a fae quint on a crucial mission. And I need to find my mates.

53

Beyond Arisha, my gaze takes in the small white-walled room with high ceilings, as if the architect attempted to balance the tiny floor space by making the walls taller. Two narrow beds, two plain wooden dressers, and two tiny desks built to fold down from the wall make up the entirety of the furniture. The thick drapes covering the one tall window might have once been bright, but now are a heavy faded olive. Beside my bed, the contents of my saddlebags spill like wine over the floor, making it difficult to find a place to step. On Arisha's side of the room, pens, paper, and books are arranged in such perfect rows, I wonder if the young woman didn't use a ruler to place them.

"You may borrow one of my uniforms for the morning exercise if you'd like." Arisha shifts her feet impatiently, chewing on her lower lip. Freckles cross her sharp cheekbones, and, beneath her round glasses, the deep bags under her eyes speak to sleeplessness or stress—or both. She is already dressed in a pair of gray pants and a matching tunic with a red insignia that must be the school's crest, both a bit small on her. Her hands shake slightly as she wrestles her long hair into two uneven braids. "It will be a little loose on your thin frame, but better than…" She waves her hand at my travel clothes, which I'd not bothered removing before bed. "Whatever you decide, you should do so quickly. Master Coal and I have an understanding that I would rather not test."

I freeze, my fingers tightening over the gray tunic

Arisha extends. "Coal?" I make myself move, changing into the offered clothes. *Coal. Coal. Coal.* "What understanding do you have with him exactly?"

"That I'm a waste of space and air that he should ignore when possible." Arisha frowns at one of her already unraveling braids. "I would like to give him every opportunity possible to continue ignoring me. Being late little helps."

Stars, Arisha truly thinks she met Coal months ago and has a whole history with the male. Autumn wasn't jesting about the power of the amulets. The complexity of magic required to build an entire intricate backstory in so many minds is enough to send a shiver down my spine.

I pull on Arisha's spare pants, using a cloth belt to keep them from falling.

She tosses me a stale roll, which I just manage to catch before it drops to the floor. "The instructors think training on an empty stomach teaches our bodies to burn fat instead of muscle and prepares us better for the 'trials of leadership.' So this is it until the midmorning meal."

"How long has, er, Master Coal, been teaching here?" I ask, shoving the roll into a pocket and hopping on one foot to get my boots back on as I follow Arisha out the door.

"Four or five months," Arisha says over her shoulder. "He came about the same time the deputy headmaster and one of the head medics did. The three of them served together on the far coast. No one in their right mind gets in Master Coal's or Commander River's way, but their medic friend is…attractive and kind, which has tripled the sick-call volume." I notice a faint blush going up Arisha's cheeks and have to swallow a curse. My males haven't just arrived—they've made an entrance.

"Is the—" I catch myself, tweaking my question before I can reveal more than I wish. "What's the medic's name?"

"Shade." Arisha stumbles as a pair of stunning women in our same drab gray uniforms brush none too gently past her. "And that would be Princess Katita and one of her favored-for-the-day ladies."

Before I can call Katita and her ilk out, the pair disappears into a sea of uniformed young cadets all flowing from their rooms to the outdoor walkways and steps. The din of conversation and boots clattering on wooden walkways mists the chilled air, my own breath turning to wisps of steam before me. Hurrying after Arisha—who is now explaining something I can't make myself pay mind to—I keep my gaze moving from face to face. I have to find the males. Quickly. Quietly. Raising no suspicion. Plans order themselves in my mind, solidifying with each step. I'll see Coal shortly. A feigned injury can take me to Shade. The veil made River a deputy headmaster. Barging into his study might be hard to explain—but hopefully the male will find me. That—

"Leralynn!" Arisha's warning hits me too late, my distraction having walked me directly into a broad muscular back.

Dressed in the same grays as I, the back's owner turns

slowly, his pine-and-citrus scent filling my nose. Amused emerald eyes look down at me from a height towering over all others, making my breath stop altogether. Thick red hair flips over a perfectly stunning, sharply angled face, one silver earring glinting.

Tye. My chest squeezes, the wave of relief washing over me so strong that I feel light-headed for a moment. I feel my hand close around Tye's wrist of its own volition. "You are here."

"Aye, lass," Tye says, glancing at where I'm still gripping his wrist. "The last I checked, I was in fact here. Are you somewhere else, then?"

Princess Katita and her friend now stop to chuckle, delicate hands covering painted lips.

I little care. Not now that I've found Tye. The half a day since I lost sight of the males is the longest we've been apart since we mated, and even with the bond itself muted in the mortal realm, the separation has left me breathless. Longing. It is a force of will to stop myself from leaping into Tye's arms, claiming his mouth before all the watching cadets.

As my eyes brush over Tye hungrily, I find myself unable to focus on his pointed ears and canines no matter how hard I try to look there, as if a great magnetic force repels my gaze. Beneath the loose folds of Tye's gray uniform, the outline of his lithe muscles are as familiar to me as his scent. As is everything about him—*almost* everything.

"Might I have my arm back now?" says Tye,

something about his voice making my gaze snap up to meet his. And once I do, I understand what's off. The lively green eyes I know so well sparkle with no sign of recognition.

8

LERA

*M*y attention sweeps to Tye's neck, the effort required to focus on where the amulet should be enough to make my head spin. When I finally manage to look, I see only the top of the male's shirt. No string. No wooden carving. Not even an impression of one beneath the cloth.

"Leralynn," Arisha hisses, pulling my hand off Tye's arm and tugging me along. "We're going to be late. Let's go."

I stumble, barely managing to stop myself from taking a nosedive down the steps. My gut clenches, the wrongness of Tye's unrecognizing gaze, his missing amulet, filling me with a new terror. Something happened in that aspen wood, something more ominous than a missed turn and misinterpreted change of course. Something that made the magic go terribly, terribly wrong.

"It's a pleasure to meet you, Leralynn," Tye calls after me, the amusement in his voice echoing off the now nearly empty dormitory walkways. Grabbing the railing, Tye vaults himself over it, jumping smoothly to the courtyard one story below. Lifting his face, he pitches his voice back up toward me. "I've other parts you can grab as well, lass, if you are so inclined."

My skin blazes, the inferno growing with the chortles of the few stragglers around me. Numb horror spreads through my limbs as I follow Arisha into the vast central square. The pale dawn sky overhead washes everything in shades of blue and gray, and it's a relief when we cross out of shadow into the slowly warming sun.

"You are insane," Arisha mutters, releasing my arm.

"Do you know who that was?" I ask, my mind sorting through the fog for possible explanations for Tye's empty eyes and finding none, except that he'd perhaps been acting. Bluffing for the sake of our cover story. Yes—a convincing act. To avoid suspicion. It has to have been.

"Everyone knows Tyelor." Arisha sighs. "The man is Great Falls Academy's top athlete, here by special invitation and preparing for the continent's Prowess Trials. Swordplay, wrestling, acrobatics—you name it, Tyelor rules it. He rules every female's attention in the place too."

"Not every female's," I say, finally focusing on Arisha's annoyed expression. "You don't like him."

She shrugs. "I'm more keen on people who can work out a defensive strategy than ones who think their ability to wave about a pointy piece of metal—or other parts—is the stars' gift to humankind." Arisha's pace quickens across the square, her shoulders hunching. "If you think you can manage stairs without killing yourself, we should try to walk faster."

Crossing under a grand stone archway and entering the training yard, which is larger than anything I've seen before, I find the place divided into a dozen grass-covered corrals. Inside each enclosure, students go through the motions of swordplay and archery, wrestling and—in the two larger arenas—horsemanship. Instructors' calls and students' grunts of effort and pain fill the morning air.

"Look for the colored flags when you come here," Arisha says, pointing to the large triangular pennants waving beside each area. "The instructors choose what training area they need for the day and mark it with their flag. We are under Coal, who has the blue flag, which is—"

"There." My voice comes out in a low whisper as my gaze falls on Coal. With black pants hanging low on his lean hips, the warrior is bare to the waist, his deadly muscles sliding beneath his skin as he demonstrates a takedown. The tattoos spiraling down the groove of Coal's spine dance as if alive with each shift of his weight. The deadly precision of that beautiful body takes my breath even now—mine, and that of the five other female students who watch the demonstration from the sidelines with similarly still chests. "That is most certainly Coal."

"You are late," the male in question calls over his shoulder as Arisha and I approach the corral. Takedown complete, Coal's attention lingers on the other students as they pair off to practice it themselves. That done, the warrior leans sideways against the fence, his arms crossed over his chest as the morning sun sculpts the hard lines of his face to menacing perfection.

"Good morning," I say quietly, the sting of Tye's greeting still shooting down my nerves. My gut clenches as I await Coal's reaction, the screaming voice in the back of my mind a reminder of how wrong everything has gone.

Coal turns at the sound of my voice and rocks back on his heels, something unreadable in his shockingly blue gaze. "I realize you're new, but I imagine you did learn to tell time before stepping foot here?"

I tense. Wait. Hold his eyes, my mind pleading for some sign of recognition. Some signal that he knows me. Knows us.

Nothing. If my body responds to the familiar danger that always vibrates inside the warrior, Coal sees nothing before him but a fresh-faced cadet.

Ice grips me at the chill in his gaze. His utter indifference to my existence.

Dipping my eyes, I trail them along Coal's body. With his shirt off and torso bare, I should be able to see the veil amulet if I know what I'm looking for, if I can conquer my body's instinct to look away from the rune-carved disk. Starting at the center of the eight hard squares of Coal's abdomen, I move my eyes along the grooved midline of his body. Up between his wide pectorals. Out along the sharp collarbones—*bloody stars,* I've strayed off course.

Forcing my eyes back to Coal's midline, I trace the groove again, refusing to look away. My head pounds, the need to focus elsewhere so palpable that it makes breathing difficult. A ringing starts in my ears, the sound and pressure growing more painful with each fraction of an inch my gaze climbs.

I dig my nails into my palm. *Look up, Lera. Up. A little more.*

It takes me a moment to realize that I've reached my target because there, at the hollow of Coal's sternum where the amulet should be, nothing hangs at all. Instead, my aching eyes trace the outlines of a circular tattoo with an ornate pointed pattern, the exact size and design the amulet would have been. As if Coal's body somehow absorbed the magical artifact. My heart pounds, recalling the flat lay of Tye's shirt. *Stars.*

"Am I inconveniencing your daydreaming?" Coal's voice snaps like a whip, drawing my attention back to his face. Cold blue eyes weigh me—and find me wanting. Just like when he first saw me all those months ago in Zake's barn. "What is your name?"

Arisha curses under her breath, quietly enough that a human wouldn't have heard.

"Creative, though not physiologically possible, I believe," Coal tells Arisha, his brow cocking toward her quickly paling face. No wonder these students are terrified of River and Coal—when you're up against preternatural fae senses without knowing it, there's nowhere to hide.

"Feel free to improve on that model as you take two laps around the Academy."

"That's over f-five miles," Arisha stutters.

"Fair point. Three laps." Coal's focus returns to me, his tone as hard as I've ever heard it. "I asked for your name, Cadet."

9

COAL

"*L*eralynn," the new student standing before Coal said, pronouncing the name as if it should mean something to him. In her early twenties, the young woman was stunning enough to stir Coal's cock, her shining auburn hair and large brown eyes reflecting the misty dawn rays. Ethereal, that was the only word for her. Even beneath an ill-fitting uniform she must have borrowed from Arisha, the swell of her breasts and the curve of her hips held the attention of every male in the training corral. Which had no right to bother Coal, though it did. Leralynn cleared her throat. "Or Lera. Or mortal."

"Mortal?" Coal echoed, the word singing to him even as the two dozen cadets of his training cadre laughed at the joke.

Lera wasn't laughing, though. She just stepped closer,

the lilac scent of her making Coal's head swim. "It's a nickname a good friend once gave me."

Coal pushed back from the fence, stepping far enough away to let the chill air clear his senses. "Your friend isn't here. Neither are your parents, your servants, your nursemaid, or anyone else who cares."

Hurt flashed across Lera's chocolate eyes. The young woman had plainly been expecting a different reception. All the new students—with their high-class upbringing and powerful family names—did. River thought shattering that particular illusion as quickly as possible was the humane approach. Coal little cared whether it was humane—he cared that it was efficient. In the five months since his assignment to Great Falls, half the students assigned to Coal's team had decided to pack up and go home within a week of arrival.

From her bewildered expression, Leralynn would be joining the departing ranks soon enough. With luck, she might complain about Coal before leaving. Make the headmaster finally decide that Coal was more trouble than he was worth. Then River would *have* to let him leave, go back to the far coast, where Coal could lick his wounds in private. If he was lucky, maybe find some new war to fight in—there was always one conflict or another with islanders. Coal had no business teaching—let alone teaching noble brats who were not much younger than his twenty-seven years, yet seemed to have lived not the quarter of the life he had.

Coal's attention returned to his newest headache,

whose mere presence was already making half the male cadets in the corral trip over their own feet. Yes, the boys had not yet learned the dangers of women.

"Well, *mortal*, do you see the three dozen stones in that corner?" Coal jerked his chin toward a pile of rough, watermelon-sized boulders arranged into a neat pile. The limestone from which they'd been cracked had a chalklike feel, the grit having an uncanny way of rubbing skin and getting under clothes. "Move them to the next corner over. And then the next."

A muscle in Leralynn's jaw ticked.

Arisha moved slowly away from them in the corner of his vision.

Coal moved closer, invading Lera's space, seizing upon the embers of anger sparking in the girl's eyes at what she no doubt saw as unjust punishment. Anger was good. It made Coal's point for him. He wasn't her friend. Didn't want to be her friend. And given the painful effect Lera's mere presence was having on his body, the sooner she walked out of his world, the better. Coal clicked his tongue. "And once you do that, move them to the next. Do you think you can remember all that without a clerk's assistance?"

"I'll endeavor to keep track of so complex a routine," she said, her voice quiet but not weak. Despite barely reaching Coal's shoulder, Lera held her ground when larger men would have retreated, the heat of her body an answering blow to Coal's challenge. Small and fierce and somehow unafraid of him. "I'll do it all twice if you leave off Arisha. She was only late on my account."

Stars take him. "Make that offer *after* you finish the circuit," Coal said, returning to the other students, who'd opportunistically stopped drilling and now watched the show with unabashed curiosity. Or, in the males' case, watched Leralynn. A glare from Coal set that to rights before he tossed his voice over his shoulder. "If you finish in time to be of any use to your friend, that is."

Instead of an answer, Coal heard the scrape of stone on stone as the small cadet heaved the first burden into her arms. And then the second. The fifth. The tenth. By the time she'd moved the load one corner over, Coal knew he'd made a strategic error: making Lera haul stones about was a punishment, but implying that her speed would determine another's fate was a challenge. How the bloody hell was he to have guessed the small spitfire would rise to it?

Even with his back to her, pretending to watch the sparring pairs before him, Coal could hear Lera's labored breathing, see the tracks in the sand where her balance faltered as she hurried faster than was wise. *Stars,* she was going to injure herself if she kept it up. And there wasn't a bloody thing he could do about it now except to witness the gambit he himself had set into motion. This wasn't about the punishment, or even Lera's friend—not really. Coal had greeted Lera with an opening volley designed to drive her away, and the bloody woman was calling him on it. And winning. Two dozen students in the corral before him, and Coal couldn't get his attention off the one walking the perimeter fence—and doing so faster than a girl her size had any right to be.

Arisha of Tallie—who belonged in a sparring ring about as much as a tabby cat belonged in a choir—was just finishing the first of her three laps when Lera planted herself in front of Coal, standing so close that he took an involuntary step back. The girl's sweat carried a sweet lilac scent, tinged with a bit of a copper tang. Blood.

He tensed, the smell spurring his heart to a gallop that took all his self-control to rein in.

"I'm finished with the first circuit, sir." Leralynn told him, her brown eyes aflame. "If you allow Arisha to return to the corral, I'll get started with the second. And if you wish, the third after that."

Grasping Lera's slender wrist, Coal twisted it palm up. The calluses from what looked like weapons training were intact, but the skin on the sensitive middle of the hand was rubbed raw. Shallow but painful wounds that roused every protective instinct in Coal's body to the surface. Which made no sense. "Your sleeves are too long." Coal's voice was flat. "If you were smart, you'd have pushed them down to cover your hands and prevented this."

"I presumed the point of the exercise was to make me miserable, so thought I might as well be efficient about it." Lera's fingers curled over her palm. "Now, are you going to hold up your end of the deal...sir?"

COAL STRODE into Shade's infirmary office, slamming the door hard enough to make the wooden frame shake in protest. "I want out," Coal said without preamble, his blood simmering as it had since morning training. "I'm a soldier, not a bloody nursemaid for noble brats."

"Do you?" In his neat white shirt and leather vest, long black hair pulled back, Shade looked every inch the civilized officer—though Coal had fought beside Shade for enough years to know the man was a vicious warrior when the situation called for it. Still, Shade seemed as content here at the Academy as when he, Coal, and River served together at the coast, fighting the hordes of islanders wanting to gain a foothold on the continent.

"I was unaware that you ever *wanted* to be here," Shade said with a hint of amusement as he rose from behind his desk and walked around to perch himself on its edge. "So, you see how the absence of the desire now fails to make an impression on me."

"I'm not here to make an impression."

Shade's strange golden eyes strayed to the door, likely assuring the lock was engaged before speaking—this time in a low voice. Shade was a friend, yes, but also Coal's military superior, a fact that Coal sensed was about to be brought up. "You are here because you were one bad night away from doing something stupid," Shade murmured. "To put it bluntly, King Zenith invested too great a fortune in your training to let you get yourself killed in some suicidal outing. Until you've worked out... whatever is going on in there, Lieutenant, you aren't going anywhere." He gestured toward Coal's head as if it were a messy barracks.

"It's worked out." Coal crossed his arms. In the five months since Coal had come here—since Shade and River had forced him here—things had only worsened. The nightmares. The flashes of darkness and groundless fear. Images of a woman who was never real to begin with, yet whose loss bled him raw. Coal's spine stiffened. He was a soldier. He needed to fight, not sit shackled behind high walls. "I'm fine, Shade. What isn't fine is this made-up world of Great Falls Academy, where brats play at soldiers and generals, safely away from anything that might actually take their lives. I want no part of it."

"I see." Shade's words barely touched the air before the man was moving, his body low, his hands snatching at Coal's unprotected elbow.

Coal shifted his weight, his mind waking to the fight. Twisting away from Shade's opening attack, he crouched low, his breath even as his eyes took in the room. Lunging forward, his hands cut Shade's knees out from under him, sending the dark-haired warrior to the floor.

Shade fell smoothly, rolling over his shoulder to reclaim his footing. Chest rising with deep breaths, he bared his teeth, his feet light as he circled Coal. With a soft growl, the man lunged forward again, this time ducking under Coal's arm to grab his wrist. With a force few people had, Shade slammed Coal's arm against the wall, his strong grip a living restraint.

Coal's stomach twisted. The world rumbled in his ears.

Giving no reprieve, Shade captured Coal's other wrist, forcing both against Coal's sides.

The rumbling in Coal's ears turned to roaring. The air seemed to flash, like lightning striking through the night, and the stench of pain and fear and blood from a dank prison cell vibrated through each fiber of his body. His heart raced, beating so hard, his ribs felt the impact. His muscles tightened, powerful and ready, his eyes widening to take in the slowing world he was about to destroy.

Because he *would* destroy it.

Pressing his shoulder blades into the wall for purchase, Coal speared his heel into his assailant's chest so hard that he felt ribs crack.

His captor flew backward, crashing into his own desk and sliding to the floor. Wood splintered, black ink spilling across paper, mixing with the thin stream of red blood dripping from the bastard's cut brow. Shade's brow.

Coal swore. Dropping to one knee beside his friend, he slid a hand behind the warrior's back, easing him into a sitting position. "Are you insane?" Coal demanded, loosening the top of the man's jacket to help him breathe. "No. Don't move about."

Drawing a hissing breath, Shade wrapped his arm around his ribs, his yellow gaze piercing Coal's. Anyone less trained would have ended up with a broken neck, but Shade knew how to take a fall. Had known what was coming before he ever attacked.

"I will give you your medical clearance to leave when you can tell the difference between friend and foe—

whether or not they are trying to restrain you." Shade's voice was tight with pain as he pressed his sleeve against the bleeding gash on his brow and frowned at the stain. "And River is fully with me on this. We've known each other for ten years, Coal. If you won't tell us what the hell those bastards who held you prisoner did to you, then find someone else to talk to. Until you figure this out, you are not going anywhere."

10

LERA

"Come. You'll feel better after you eat. Maybe." Shepherding me along, Arisha leads me into the dining hall, where high-backed cushioned chairs surround ornately carved wooden tables, each seating groups of four to eight quietly murmuring students. The shining marble floors reflect grand crystal candelabras hanging from the vaulted ceiling, the candles unlit in deference to the sun streaming in through tall, spotless windows. Fine woven runners in rich reds and blues mark the pathways between tables. The gray uniforms look as out of place here as ball gowns in a stable. "The dining hall is informal the first half of the day," Arisha explains, "but we dress up for dinner."

I nod, not trusting my voice. My breaths come heavy still, my muscles trembling from fatigue. My fae body will heal faster than a human's would, but I still hurt. The physical pain is the least of my worries just now, though. Like Tye, Coal didn't recognize me, didn't so much as glance my way the entire time I worked. Not an act. Where does that leave our mission, then? Do the males remember why we are at the Academy at all? Does *River*, our commander, remember?

Something went wrong after we parted ways on the forest path, and until I can get one of them alone, I have no way of knowing the extent of it. I shiver, remembering Coal's icy gaze. No connection, no attraction, not even a curiosity. As if what I believed were unbreakable bonds of love are nothing more than a trick of magic. A house of cards that, with that magic's disappearance, has simply collapsed.

Finding an empty table, Arisha motions for me to sit while she fetches two portions of hearty porridge and heels of steaming fresh bread, relief at training's end hanging around her like a cloud. Even after Coal allowed her to stop running, Arisha had done poorly in practice, tripping over her own feet so often that Coal finally set her aside to work basic punches against thin air. She'd fallen doing that too.

"Coal always goes hard on new people," Arisha says, pushing the bowl closer to me. "Don't take it personally. Though maybe negotiating with Coal on my behalf wasn't exactly the best strategic move."

I blink, forcing myself to concentrate on her words. "I was the one who made you late. You were kind to wait for me when I—when we met Tyelor this morning." I lean closer to the porridge, letting the warm scent ground me, and realize suddenly that I haven't eaten a real meal since our noon break yesterday. Somehow, that feels like days ago. A different lifetime in which my males surrounded me, jesting with each other, running a hand over my hair or lower back on their way past. My throat tightens. "Fair is fair."

"Not here." Arisha's freckled cheeks tighten. "In fact, once you know your way around better, you'd be better off not sitting with me at all. Everyone knows the physical training will force me out sooner or later, and you should be working toward better alliances."

"I'll make up my own mind if it's all the same to you," I tell Arisha, hissing as I pick up my spoon. The abrasions on my palms aren't deep, but they sting.

"Well, if I've not found my two new favorite lasses," Tye says, putting his tray down on the small table right after a heady citrus-and-pine scent fills my nose. Pulling a chair out for himself, he turns it around and straddles it in a smooth motion, his attention fully on Arisha. "I need a favor, braids."

The small kernel of hope that I dared feel dies in my chest.

"And at least half the students in Great Falls would happily trip over themselves to grant you your heart's desires," Arisha tells him, her too-keen eyes taking in my reaction. "So go bother them."

Tye flashes her a smile. "Aye, but see, it is the kind of

favor *you* are best at—the mathematics kind. With numbers. And symbols. And counting."

"Counting? Well, I'd certainly not expect you to go beyond twenty on your own." Arisha tilts her head, her fingers worrying her left braid. The loose hair sticks out wildly enough to make the girl competitive for a scarecrow position. "What's in it for me?"

"Whatever you wish." Tye scoots his chair closer to her. "I can fetch your food while you work, massage your shoulders…get you a hair ribbon or ten."

Arisha moves her chair away. "I help you with your math homework. You help Leralynn with her hands." My eyes widen, but Arisha avoids my gaze, her attention now wholly on her food. "Given the amount of time you spend twirling around a stick for applause, you must know what to do with that." She waves in my direction.

"What happened?" Tye turns toward me, his long lashes and sharply angled face so painfully beautiful that I hate myself for my own heart's stutter. For how much my body longs for the warrior's touch, even knowing it's spurred by nothing but the rules of Arisha's transaction. *Stars.* I'm better than this. I hope I'm better than this.

"Coal happened." I pull my hands onto my lap. "And I don't need help. Thank you, though."

Reaching over the table with his long arms, Tye snatches my wrist impertinently. "Sorry, lass, but I'm not risking failing mathematics. They'll bar me from competing." Placing the back of my wrist onto the tabletop, the male opens my fingers gently, drawing a small breath as he assesses the damage with a knowing gaze. "Was it a rope?" Tye asks, the concern in his voice the first genuine thing I've heard since meeting him here.

"No."

Tye's emerald eyes flicker up to mine.

I study a rip in my sleeve.

"A secret. I like those." Dipping a corner of his linen napkin into a water glass, Tye dabs gently against the cuts, his grip on my wrist tightening when I try to pull away. "Hold on, lass. We need to wash the sand out before this turns from nuisance to corruption."

We. The word pierces me. Lifting my face, I find Tye absorbed in his work, those sharply angled cheekbones with their constellation of nearly invisible freckles tightened in concentration, one lock of red hair falling over his forehead, his hand as warm against the back of mine as if his fire magic had brushed the skin. I try not to soak him in too obviously, but it's desperately hard. Tye wets the napkin again, his rolled-up sleeves showing off his muscled arms.

I brace myself for the sting.

Tye pauses. This time, instead of bringing the cloth directly to my palm, he runs his thumb firmly over my forearm.

I gasp softly, my sore muscles singing at the exquisite pressure that radiates up my arm.

"Be good and I'll do that again," Tye murmurs, a corner of his mouth twitching.

"I—"

"Tyelor." The unexpected sound of River's voice makes my heart jump, then race like a rabbit.

Turning, I find River standing beside our table, the aura of command hanging about him with familiar ease. Back straight, River holds his hands behind him, his well-cut red coat buttoned high up his neck.

11

LERA

*A*risha and Tye rise at once, and by the time I follow their example a few moments later, the two are already bowing.

"Good morning, sir," Arisha and Tye say together, just as I mouth, *River*.

River's beautiful gray eyes slide over me with enough scrutiny to tighten my chest—and no familiarity. Although I was little expecting it by now, its absence still stings. "Your servant, ma'am," River says dryly. "I presume I've the pleasure of addressing Lady Leralynn of Osprey, who managed to break curfew last night and get on the wrong side of an instructor this morning?" River's keen gaze flickers over my hands, the distance between us widening with each passing breath. He's painfully handsome and somehow even taller and more imposing than I remember, as if we've spent years apart already.

"Yes," I answer, searching his eyes for something —anything.

A pause. Pregnant. Waiting.

"*Sir,*" Tye murmurs to me.

Bloody stars. "Yes, sir," I tell River.

River nods. "Despite its grander-than-life reputation, Great Falls Academy is in truth a poor fit for a significant number of would-be students, Lady Leralynn." River's schooled gaze studies me with all the passion of a glass vase. "As such, I highly encourage anyone who finds our rules and customs unpalatable to depart sooner rather than later."

My throat closes, my mind trying and failing to overlay this official with the male who took me in my bedchamber two days ago. I reach inside myself on instinct, searching for the mating bond before remembering the amulets' effects on it. Amulets that all four of my males were wearing when I took mine off to gallop toward the odd call of magic. My mind races, wanting to follow this trail, but Arisha nudges me, and I realize with a start that I've never replied to River's...invitation to get out of his life.

Shoving all thought and feelings into the darkness of my mind, I raise my chin at the deputy headmaster, who wears a soldier's epaulets and a familiar face.

"Understood, sir." My voice is clear and uncowed, mirroring nothing of my soul. The voice I cultivated under Zake, where signs of weakness led to pain. "I will apply myself to learning swiftly."

River nods again, dismissing the new student as a

nuisance while his attention shifts to Tye, whom he'd originally approached to see. The commander's already wide shoulders spread further, encroaching on the other's space without him ever taking a step. "A valuable medallion pendant has disappeared from my office, Tyelor," River says, his voice low. "Would you happen to know anything about it?"

Well, Autumn did say the veil amulets drew what they could from true history—and a good portion of Tye's was spent in and out of arrest. If I wasn't ready to scream in frustration, I might actually chuckle.

"I don't think so, sir." Tye cocks his head, feline impertinence in every lithe line of his beautiful body. "What did it look like?"

"A disk. The size of a small saucer. With designs inscribed."

Any trace of amusement drains from me. The key to Mystwood—that's what River describes. Our one and only way of getting home. Gone. And beyond believing it a valuable trinket, I don't think River even knows what he lost. The chill rushing over my skin turns to ice. The tear in the fabric, the threat to the mortal realm—none of it went away with my males' lost memories. And now I can't even travel back to summon aid.

"Hmm." Tye rocks back on his heels. "I've seen nothing of the sort, sir. But I will certainly keep my eyes open for it."

River steps forward, towering even over Tye. "If you locate it, please inform the culprit that thievery will not be tolerated at Great Falls. From anyone. No matter how many medals they've won. Have I made myself clear?"

Tye blinks, spreading his hands in innocence. "Of course, sir. As it shouldn't be."

River steps back, his eyes brushing me again, the smooth planes of his face impassive. Frowning, he focuses on my neck, as if he can see the veil amulet there. My breath halts, my body going still. *Do you see something, River? Do you remember who I am?*

The male crooks a finger at me.

I approach obediently, my heart beating a thready quick beat under his relentless gaze. *See me, River. Feel me.*

As I stop before him, River stretches his hand toward my neck. Toward—

"Jewelry is not permitted with gray uniforms," he says, and I realize his intention to pull the amulet off. My hands rise defensively, my head shaking in desperate protest that River ignores as his fingers wrap around the pendant and pull. The chain digs into the back of my neck as it breaks.

Holding my breath, I wait for the gasps and panic, the shock as my disguise comes crashing down around me, its careful preservation the only thing that's been preventing me from hauling my males out by the shirt collars and forcing them to remember me. But nothing comes. Blinking, I finally focus my eyes on exactly what River pulled from my neck and tossed like a bit of rubbish onto the tabletop. Not the veil amulet, but the intricate four-corded necklace he gifted me with the morning we left Lunos.

"It can cause injury during training," he says, already moving away. "You may wear jewelry only with formal dress."

I breath in the mix of relief and hurt, using the time it takes to sweep the broken gift into my pocket to reclaim my schooled face. "Did you take River's pendant?" I ask Tye once I'm certain the other male is well out of earshot. Tye—*my* Tye—very well might have, for the amusement of it if nothing else. But the male before me knows nothing of his own roguish history in Lunos.

Tye grins. "Actually, I've no notion what River was talking about. But if I find it, I've some idea how much it's worth now, aye?"

WE RETURN to Coal for more training after breakfast and dive into the academic components of Great Falls' famous education in the afternoon. This opens another gaping problem. Raised as a stable hand, I learned my letters from a kind older servant who took me under her wing. The difference between basic reading and strategic analysis, however, is as vast as the rift between realms. The veil amulet might have convinced the teachers I belong in their class, but it can't compensate for the fact that I understand nothing of what's placed before me. Especially when I'm busy trying to work a way out of this mess.

Pulling a shawl tight around my ornate silver dress— Arisha prompted me to change for dinner after classes ended, having the decency to only raise a single brow when I pulled out one of Autumn's ridiculously royal creations—I step into the library where Arisha, Tye, and I are to meet up for study that I'll understand none of. The deeply carved wooden doors open into a great round room with a domed red-and-gold ceiling, the walls lined so high up with shelves of books that ladders stand beside them to help pull down the volumes. The trove of information surrounding me hums with the reminder of what I'm missing. How much I don't know about what happened to my males—and need to figure out. Quickly.

I realize my hands are shaking and sink into the first high-backed chair I find, grateful to have arrived early. It's the first quiet moment I've had to think since waking up here at dawn. My mouth is dry, my heart beating a thin pattering rhythm against my ribs, my stomach hollow despite the lavish spread of healthy food at dinner. Leafy salads and roasted root vegetables and poached chicken breasts. Even the perfectly seasoned risotto tastes like dust in my mouth. Bracing my elbows on the table before me, I cradle my aching head and force myself to sort through the disaster again.

The males and I were approaching Academy grounds... The images swim in my head.

No. I approached alone, clutching the Academy invitation that freed me from Lord Zake of Osprey, who took me in as his ward.

No. No, that isn't right.

There is no Osprey.

Of course there is, I spent my childhood there.

86

The ache in my head turns to painful pounding with each beat of my heart.

I was traveling in the forest.

No, on the main road of course. Like a proper lady.

No.

"Are you quite all right?" asks a male voice a few feet away. Blinking up, I find a man in dark olive robes rising from behind the library's main desk. In his late fifties, the librarian has a well-tutored voice, light brown hair peppered with gray, and thick glasses. Leaning on a cane to assist his stiff left leg, he makes his way toward my table, his eyes examining me with uncomfortable intensity as he touches my shoulder. "You appear pale, my lady. And new."

I shift away and the man's hand drops from my shoulder, the loss of contact burning my flesh in reminder of my males' absence. *Stars,* I'm like a stray dog desperate for touch. "I'm well. Just a bit overwhelmed." I stand, starting for the door. "Excuse me."

My mind swims again. *I can't leave—I need to study, lest the Academy sends me back to Lord Zake in disgrace.* No.

"Wait." The man takes a step toward me. "My name is Gavriel. I'm the Academy's librarian. What is your name?"

"Lady Leralynn of Osprey," I mutter.

Gavriel sighs, running his hand through his hair the same way that...that someone I once knew did when anxious. "I believe you need to take the veil off for a spell."

"Your pardon?" I ask over the pounding in my skull. My hands touch my face, finding only skin. "What veil?"

Gavriel curses and limps around me, his cane making an efficient *tick tick tick* against the marble floor. Stopping behind me, he brushes the back of my neck, a small click of a lock sounding before I can pull away.

The pounding in my head stops at once, my thoughts clearing as I feel the amulet slipping down into my hand, the intricately carved runes on its wooden face as cold as ice.

"There we are." Gavriel limps quickly to the library door, sliding the latch closed. "Feeling better?"

12

LERA

"*Who* are you?" My voice skitters off the rounded library walls.

"Gavriel," he repeats simply, inclining his head to me as he pulls a chair out for himself and sits, massaging his knee. "Currently the librarian at Great Falls."

"And at other times?" I press.

"A cardinal of the Sentinel Guild, keeping watch over the mortal realm."

I sink slowly into my chair, my hand clutching the veil amulet. *Stars.* With everything that's happened, I'd forgotten to remove it as Autumn instructed—with near disastrous results. Now, without the magical artifact hanging around my neck, the headache and confusion are easing quickly—though even that little helps comprehend Gavriel's presence. I focus on his ears, expecting my gaze

89

to slip away as it does with the males, but find no problem looking at him.

"I am human," Gavriel confirms. "And you are fae."

I swallow. "But the veil amulet had no effect on you."

"It had full effect, or I'd have found you earlier."

"But—"

"I've been expecting you, Leralynn. And I had to trust my deductions over what my own eyes and mind insisted I was seeing. As I've been trained to do." Gavriel pulls a pendant from beneath his robes, showing it off as if the symbol of pen and shield should mean something to me. Seeing that it doesn't, he sighs and tucks the disk away. "Perhaps I should start at the beginning. After the ancients separated the mortal lands from Lunos, the humans feared that with our limited life span, the truth would morph and wither. The Sentinel Guild guards the history, studies the present, and stands watch should the divide ever be breached—for good or ill."

"By *stands watch* you mean—" I say.

Gavriel nods. "We keep the knowledge alive."

I rub my face. "In other words, you are a walking reference text of events so long past that no one else gives a damn about them anymore?" I wince. "My apologies. I could have worded that better."

Gavriel adjusts his glasses. "Yes. And... yes." He motions to a thick volume resting on the edge of his desk, and I oblige the silent request, bringing the book over to him. "The twist to your humor being that my guild's work has proven correct—as evidenced by my having anticipated your coming. And yes, I will explain that in a moment as well."

He flips through the book, his attention on the pages. "Have you heard the legend about fae coming through from the other lands to take a worthy warrior and grant him eternal life?"

"I have. Zake, the lord I used to be indentured to, told it often—mostly because he believed himself to be the chosen one. The man was so stars bent on it that he built a whole estate at Mystwood's edge, waiting for immortality to summon him." I wrap my arms around myself, the memories pricking like tiny needles. "The irony was that fae warriors *did* show up at Zake's estate, except for a different reason."

"The Sentinel's Guild would take issue with your word choice, Leralynn," Gavriel says.

"Which word?"

"Irony." He turns the book he's holding around, the pictures showing a human turning fae in stages, ears rising, body and hair lengthening, a sword held high in her hands. The next image over shows the same grand hero protecting a village from shadowed hordes. "We prefer prophecy."

I stare at Gavriel, waiting for the laugh, but the man is serious. "You think that I—" I shake my head. "The fae didn't summon me to Lunos to gift me with immortal life, Gavriel. That was more an accidental by-product of my death."

"And yet here you are." The man opens his hands, his

brown eyes round with excitement. "Born in the mortal world, summoned to Lunos, returning as an immortal warrior yourself—right when and where beasts of wrongness and corruption have begun raising their heads." Gavriel closes the book. "That is why I took the position at Great Falls, if you were wondering. After hearing of fae taking a mortal near Mystwood, I sought out reports of unusual incidents—which Great Falls has seen a bit of in the past months. My prediction was that you'd return as an immortal warrior right in the center of the fray. I was not wrong. A battle is coming, and you are here to defend our kind, Leralynn. With me here to guide you through it, the best I am able."

I'm speechless for a moment, unsure whether to laugh hysterically or scream. "Bloody stars, Gavriel. You are as insane as Zake." My headache creeps back even without the amulet, and I squeeze my temples to avoid shaking him. "Listen to me. I'm not a lone hero returned to battle beasts untold. I'm here as part of a five-warrior quint ordered to find and seal a crack in the wards protecting the mortal realm from magic."

For the first time since walking into the library, I see Gavriel's scholarly face rippling with confusion. "Five-warrior quint? No. No, that can't be right." He huffs. "That wasn't in the prophecy. These texts have been studied and deciphered by the kingdom's greatest minds. The Protector comes alone."

"Then we both agree I'm not the Protector you are waiting for." I force my voice under control and lean toward him with the most polite demeanor I can manage. "But if you could see your way to using all those centuries of knowledge to help me find a way out of the mess I'm actually in, I'd be most obliged. Yesterday, River, Coal, Shade, Tye, and I were approaching the Academy when I heard a static-like noise. I took off my amulet to investigate, but my horse tripped over what seemed to be an old rune-covered tablet. There was a flash, and I was unconscious for some time. When I finally made my way to the Academy, I discovered that the males now actually believe the veil amulet's legends. I need to get their memories back. Can you help?"

Gavriel stares at me, his mouth working without sound.

I wait, holding his gaze and my breath.

After a few heartbeats, the man shakes himself and pulls a sheet of handwritten notes from inside his breast pocket. "There have been reports of wild animal assaults from some of Great Falls's farms, but what I've been able to glean suggests beasts from another realm," Gavriel says as if I'd not spoken at all. "Skysis—"

"Sclices."

"Ah, sclices. I will make the correction. I believe sclices to be the culprits and have outlined the details here. This should be our first line of attack." He slides the sheet over to me and takes off his glasses, polishing them intently on his wool robe. "Since the prophecy mentions nothing of companions, there is no cause to focus there."

"Wait, what?" I blink. Rub my eyes. Blink again.

"Gavriel… I little care what the prophecy says. I care about reversing what happened to my quint so we can continue with our very *real* and very *urgent* mission." A mission, I realize, which my males remember no more than they recall the veil amulets or sclices or anything else they've encountered over centuries in Lunos. "Do you…do you understand what I'm trying to say at all?"

His jaw tightens. "If your companions were important, the prophecy would have mentioned them. And given the rather prominent Academy personnel you are naming, it is entirely possible that their role in this affair is to be played out from their current personas. We need to focus on protecting the mortal realm. Nothing else."

"I don't think there is a *we,* then." Rising to my feet, I clip the veil amulet back onto my neck and start for the door.

"There is something else you should know," Gavriel calls after me. "Your old master has been stirring up fuss about fae, accusing the immortals of everything from replacing healthy babes with ill ones to killing livestock, and worse. It's taken hold—hate, I fear, is rather easy to spread."

"I grew up next to Mystwood," I say without turning. "Tales of murderous fae are nothing new to me."

"No." Gavriel's voice sharpens. "I speak not of legends and children's tales of far-off beasts. Zake and his inquisitors are arresting people on charges of being fae blood carriers and sympathizers. By the time they are done questioning or cleansing or whatever name they give torture nowadays, there is usually little left but a confession. And execution."

I shake my head. "There are no fae in the mortal lands, bar the five of us. And we came just a day ago."

"I'm certain the families of five hundred of Zake's victims will be pleased to hear that," says Gavriel.

"Why are you telling me this?" I ask, ice gripping my chest as tightly as I grip the doorknob.

"So you know what is likely to happen if you yank off your amulet in front of the Academy's deputy headmaster, as I believe you might consider doing. Either that, or accuse River, Coal, Shade, Tye, or anyone else of fae craft."

13

LERA

I rush out of the library into the long, torch-lit hallway so quickly that I crash into Tye for the second time that day. The male's pine-and-citrus scent alerts me to his identity a moment before his firm, warm hands steady my elbows. I resist the urge to press into his hard chest, though every instinct in my body tells me I belong there.

"Are you all right?" Arisha asks with wide blue eyes, holding her armful of books closer to her chest. "Is there something in there?"

"Yes. Stupid ideas," I mutter, though not quietly enough to get past Tye's keen hearing.

Throwing his head back, the male laughs, the sound rich and easy. Releasing me much earlier than I wish, he sticks his hands into his pockets, the movement shifting his vest to reveal an embroidered shirt beneath the velvet. The rich blue-and-gold crest of the Prowess Trials—the Alliance's grand competition of strength and agility— winks at me from the fabric. In Lunos, Tye was once heading for authentic glory, until a jealous prince forced him to abandon the life dream. Now it seems the amulet is giving Tye another chance.

"How old are you, Tye?" I blurt, speaking over whatever Tye or Arisha were about to say next.

He blinks once. "Twenty-two."

Bloody hell take me. "What do you think of fae?" I press on, little caring for how odd the question sounds. My heart beats fast and shallow against my ribs. I need to know whether Gavriel's assessment of the danger is true. And I need to know quickly.

Tye cocks his right brow, his wickedly handsome face and green eyes taking on a mischievous tinge. "I think anyone immortal likely has access to old expensive things. And I think I can make good use of such items. Is there one sitting in the library?"

"Tyelor," Arisha hisses at him. "That is not amusing."

"You only think so because you can't see your own face just now." Tye opens his eyes wide in a fair imitation of Arisha before returning his gaze to me, the humor fading. "Word about fae is that a small gang of the bastards came through Mystwood and kidnapped a virgin last year—and more have crept in since to do murder and worse. Does no good gossip reach Osprey?"

"You don't actually believe that, do you?" I ask. "About fae being evil, I mean, not gossip's travel patterns."

"Don't know either way, and it doesn't matter. Braids here is right." Tye tugs on Arisha's hair, making the woman scowl. "Talking about fae craft is a great way to end up on an inquisitor's table having your joints measured for length. And whispering of it on Academy grounds—even theoretically—is a sure way to end up in River's study." Tye takes a step toward me, his voice dropping dramatically. "Which means you are a dangerous woman already."

You have no idea.

"Are you two going to study or exchange taunts?" Arisha demands, tucking her braids out of harm's reach.

I pull my shawl tighter around my shoulders. "Neither for me, I'm afraid. It's been a bit of a trying first day, and I'm turning in early. Please enjoy mathematics without my company." I hurry down the broad stone steps outside before either can ask questions, pausing only to call over my shoulder, "If you are such an impressive athlete, Tye, you could carry Arisha's books, you know."

"The lass won't let me," Tye calls after me. "Apparently, I'm not to be trusted with such precious artifacts."

The light notes of Tye's voice haunt me all the way back to my bedchamber, where I shut the door and slide my back down it until I'm sitting on the cold floor. My hands tremble, and I force myself to take deep, even breaths the way Coal—my Coal—would have told me to do now. This whole mess isn't prophecy. It's a mistake. An accident. A by-product of a magical relic shattering beneath a running horse's hooves.

No, not *shattered*. I jerk to my feet, my mind racing. The relic was never shattered, just cracked. The pieces might still be reassembled into a whole. If I can find my way back to where it all happened before weather covers the tracks or wrecks the softer insides of the tablet.

Crossing the room, I survey the settling evening through my large window. I'll have to wait until darkness before standing a chance of going over the Academy wall undetected. Whether the night's full moon and my immortal eyes will prove enough to let me follow my own tracks back to the forked road where it all started remains to be seen. At worst, I'll have to wait out in the woods until sunrise. Either way, it's a plan. After a day stuck in my disguise, going through the motions, it's action. And that makes me feel better.

I change from my dress into a dark suit of soft leather I'd brought from Lunos, getting myself ready and under the covers before Arisha returns to the darkened room. The woman whispers my name and, upon discovering me seemingly asleep, makes quick and quiet work of getting into bed herself. A quarter hour later, her soft steady breathing fills the bedchamber.

I hope you are a heavy sleeper, Arisha, I mouth shortly after the Academy's bell tolls ten-o'clock curfew. Swinging myself out of bed, I sheathe my blade down the length of my spine and tuck Shade's mittens into my belt. Using a few drops of oil from the lock-picking kit, I lubricate the window hinges before swinging them open into the cold crisp night.

The fifteen-foot drop to the ground makes my stomach tighten, but there is little help for it since the door leads to the central square courtyard, where a pair of the Academy's guardsmen stand watch. Plus, having seen Tye make a similar jump this morning for the sheer showiness of it, I know it can be done. Not letting myself fret over it further, I throw my legs over the window ledge, dangle in the air, and let go.

My legs flex, taking my weight as I land on the soft earth and curse. The jump didn't break my legs, but I did nearly twist an ankle. A fae body is a nice thing, but without the centuries of training the males have, it will be a long time yet before I can use its full ability. Coal had been working with me on that before we left. *Coal.* My heart squeezes.

Drawing a few deep breaths, I turn about to examine my surroundings. The backdrop of trees stares back at me, the Academy eerily quiet in the darkness. Closing my eyes, I press into a great oak's shadow and listen. It truly isn't fair how much I can hear the humans, their measured steps along the cobblestone paths on the other side of the dormitory, their softly exchanged reports. Curt, professional words of a well-trained guard force.

Great Falls Academy is not taking any chances with security. *River* is not taking any chances. Except for the one he knows nothing about.

Taking a breath, I move deeper into the buffer of

wilderness separating the Academy's core complex from the protective wall around it, a moat of oaks and pines concealing the tall stone eyesore from sight. I marked one of those oaks earlier, with its sturdy branches and close-to-the-wall location, as my exit point. Silvery moonlight slants down through the branches, giving me just enough light. Not an easy climb, but doable. And certainly better than trying to talk my way past the guards at the gate. Finding the tree, I rub my hands over the wide trunk.

"I wouldn't do that." The self-satisfied voice purrs so close to my ear that my heart jumps inside my ribs. Tye may not know he's fae, but he certainly kept both his instincts and feline impertinence when the veil settled over him. "You'll get yourself caught faster than you can say 'get lost, Tyelor gorgeous.'"

Heart still pounding, I twist to find Tye leaning against the tree next to mine, his muscled arms crossed over his leather-clad chest. Emerald eyes glowing in the moonlight slide up over my hips and breasts before finally settling on my face, the predatory glint in them so familiar that it hurts, for there is no recognition lurking behind it.

"What are you doing here?" I demand.

"Saving you from a fairly severe thrashing, by the looks of it." Tye jerks his chin from the tree to the wall. "Do you imagine you're the first to discover this oak's convenient location? There's going to be a guard near here any moment. If you want to get over the wall—and I am rather curious as to what you think you're going to find there—you'll have to work a little harder for it."

"And you've an idea of a better path?" I ask. Whether the veil imparted Tye with such knowledge or the rogue's trained eye deduced it on instinct, I trust the male's criminal-mindedness over my own any day.

"Aye." Tye stretches lazily, pausing in midmotion, his head cocking attentively to one side. When I open my mouth to ask what he's marking, Tye clamps his palm over it, his other arm jerking me against his chest. "Shhhh. Behind us." Tye's lips are so close to my ear, the whispered words tickle, his warmth and breathing steady against my back. "I told you the guards patrol this all the time. This way."

14

RIVER

*R*iver laid the latest grim report on Headmaster Sage's desk and stepped back, putting his hands into the small of his back. Great Falls Academy held to the military protocol and, like River himself, Headmaster Sage was a lifelong soldier. That was where the similarity ended. With thin shoulders, a gleaming bald pate, and pointed features that seemed stuck in a permanent pinch, Sage led his troops from behind paper and ink. "That is the fifth unexplained attack in a week, sir, and three dead," River said, inclining his head. "Should we send the students home until—"

"Of course not. If you've lost your mind, sir, please be good enough to inform me in writing." Leaning back in his chair, Sage studied the reports, his sour expression hardening.

River knew what the smaller man was reading. Assault

after assault, with culprits named as everything from wild animals to bandits to fae spirits. So far, all the misadventures remained outside the Academy walls, the attacks occurring on the farms and the small town near the estate. But it kept happening.

Sage shook his head, stacking the reports into a perfectly neat pile to match all the other neat piles in his office. Even the logs in the crackling fireplace had been laid out in strict parallels. "The Academy's stronghold has stood for two hundred years. Shutting our doors will destroy everything King Zenith has worked for."

As well as destroy Sage's career. But that little needed to be said.

"With due respect, sir," River said, his voice a calm contrast to Sage's heated tone. "If we lose a student to whatever wild beasts are hunting these grounds, the Academy's reputation would suffer a worse blow."

"I was under the impression that student safety was the reason I brought you here to begin with, Captain River. I have already issued instructions prohibiting the cadets from leaving Academy walls. Am I to understand that you find yourself unable to keep them to such basic discipline?" The man flicked the air with his hand. "If so, I urge you to make an example of one, and the rest will lie as quiet as the sheep they are."

Not the description River would have applied to any of the Academy students, but there was nothing to be gained by arguing that point. More importantly, River wished to give Sage no reason to demonstrate his methods.

In a microcosm of two hundred would-be generals, keeping a bit firmly in the cadets' mouths was paramount; abusing them under the flag of the Academy's authority was an entirely different matter. Sage would toe the line with Zenith's daughter Katita and the other royalty, but the offspring of lesser nobles would have no such protection.

Pulling out a handkerchief, Sage coughed wetly. "Meanwhile, see if you can't find the town's wandering monster. Once you get your hands dirty, I predict you'll discover these menacing assaults coming from no more than an overactive wolf or two. If not for this bloody chill, I'd take care of it myself."

Striding out of Sage's office into the keep's long torch-lit corridor, River called on one of the pages to find Coal and Shade—the only two men he intended to take on the night's outing. Sage might not have intended for him to go tonight, but River wouldn't wait another minute with the safety of Great Falls at risk. The page, a small lad nicknamed Rabbit, paled at once, giving River a dubious look over a promise that Coal would not smite him on sight.

Coal had that effect on people, River thought, heading down a long spiraling staircase. On most people. Though Coal's latest charge, Leralynn of Osprey, appeared to have missed the announcement. The young woman would no doubt discover her oversight—to her peril.

River paused, gripping the railing as sudden nausea rolled over him. The new cadet looked so like River's late wife that he'd nearly grabbed her. Eyes the color of liquid chocolate, lush auburn hair, a self-assured confidence teetering on impertinence that no doubt got her in trouble more often than not. After a quick glance to ensure he was, in fact, alone on the stairs, River let himself sag against the rail for a moment as he rubbed his face. He'd been the one to gift Diana with the mare that threw her to her death. River, who had vowed to protect her with his life, had failed.

The bitter irony of it all was that River had accepted the position at Great Falls to get away from memories of Diana, and here was her ghost walking back into his life.

TWO HOURS LATER, with the Academy bedded down for the night, River led Coal and Shade out of the compound's main gate. Dressed in his signature black, Coal was a specter against the night, only his blond hair pulled up into a warrior's bun providing any relief from the darkness. A darkness that the warrior's eyes echoed too—had ever since he escaped captivity. What exactly happened to Coal when the islanders took him during that ill-fated scouting trip two years ago, River didn't know. Not even a direct order to speak of it had worked, and River knew better than to try again.

The Academy's guards cadre were competent enough, but nothing equated to the battlefield experience River shared with the two warriors. Plus, whatever was truly terrorizing the town and farms, Sage wanted the details kept quiet. River had to agree with that. If the Academy was to remain open as usual, then they needed to control the gossip.

Beside Coal, Shade moved with a predatory lupine grace that made him one of the most dangerous warriors on a battlefield—though the man's heart lay in healing, not killing. The assignment to Great Falls was supposed to help fill that need, and here River was, dragging him right back out into patrol. "If you've other obligations this evening—" River cut himself off at Shade's curt shake of the head.

"Nothing worth missing a hunt over." The warrior's yellow eyes shone. Good. Shade checked the blade sheathed down the length of his spine. "Where do you want me?"

Surveying the moonlit forest, River considered the question. "All the assaults have happened at night, so I believe we are dealing with something nocturnal. We split to circle the wall first, ensure no immediate threat, then reconnect to head toward the farmland and set up on the livestock."

Shade nodded once, melting silently into the woods. Sometimes River wondered if the male wasn't part wolf himself for how he prowled through the forest, the smells and darkness of night seeming to free something inside him.

"If you're this worried, why not send the students home for cause?" Coal asked, moving off in the opposite direction of Shade. "Say they couldn't master the curriculum."

"Politics." River shook his head, his gaze moving as he fell in step beside Coal. "Explaining why we forced one kingdom's subject out over another will look biased no matter what. All expulsions must be self-selected."

Coal snorted. "Give me a name of anyone you want sent home and I'll have her signing paperwork by day's end."

"Her?" River knew he should stop talking, but his treacherous mouth defied him. "Would you be thinking of your new student in particular?"

Coal's eyes remained on the woods. "I was not. But if you mean Leralynn of Osprey, she'll pack her bags quickly. I know the type." Coal shifted, drawing a boot dagger into his free hand. "Center of the world, expecting recognition the instant they draw breath in a room—and damn well getting it from every male within range." The last came as a quiet afterthought that made River's jaw tighten in the darkness.

15

LERA

*W*ith his hand on the small of my back, Tye moves on silent feet along the woods lining the wall, keeping to the darkest patches as we stray farther and farther from the barracks. Try as I may to follow the turns and twists, the grounds—already unfamiliar in daylight—are utterly unidentifiable dressed in cast shadows. The grass is dry with cold, crackling softly around my boots, and the cool air is sharp with the smell of earth and pine. After a quarter hour's stealth, the male motions for me to stop and crouches next to a set of hedges that look no different from the dozens of others. A few heartbeats later, his hand brushes dirt away from a trapdoor, which opens obediently on well-oiled hinges.

I stare into liquid darkness beneath us. "An underground passage?"

Tye nods, swinging himself down into the abyss

without ceremony. When I let myself dangle off the edge to follow him down, I discover my legs are unable to touch the ground. I clench my teeth. Tye jumped from the second story for the enjoyment of it this morning, so his easy descent tells me nothing about the floor I cannot see. The ankle I nearly twisted getting out of my window whines with fear. I draw a shaking breath, my hands aching from the strain as I try to talk myself into letting go.

Firm hands grip my calves, pulling in clear command. Tye's spotting touch echoes through me, the relief so palpable that I let my grip slide on sheer trust. The instant I do, my body drops into the male's waiting arms, which close around me protectively.

For a moment, I stay there, my face pressed into Tye's shoulder, drinking in his warmth and fresh scent. The steady rise and fall of his broad, muscled chest is soothing enough to stop time itself, returning me back to a world where the male held me readily with heart and soul. It's so familiar here, I can almost forget for a moment that everything's changed.

Unbidden, the desire to tell Tye everything fills my lungs. *You are fae, Tye. My mate. And though you remember nothing of it and think you've a life here, it's all different.* I bite my lip. Would I believe such a tale? No. No one sane would. Gavriel's warning of what fae craft accusations lead to nowadays sends a chill down my neck. This disaster with the veil amulets needs actions, not words. It needs a magical tablet to be found and fixed.

Setting me on my feet, Tye steps away and pulls down on a rope. The trap door closes obediently above us. "It's an escape tunnel," he says, leading the way forward along the rough stone. "Not very posh, but it will get us to the other side of the wall. Keep your hand on the rock to steady your bearing."

I obey, stepping gingerly, my immortal eyes making out no more than an occasional glimpse of a wall—a human would see not even that.

"The guards don't monitor this?" My foot steps on what feels like a dead rat lying in the middle of the path. I inhale sharply before moving on.

"We're passing near the main gates now, actually," Tye whispers. "There is a place in the guardhouse where they can see any light passing through here. So long as we light no candle or lantern, the risk is minimal." Tye's silhouette seems to glance over his shoulder. "But minimal isn't the same as zero, pretty lass. Are you still certain that whatever it is you want to do is worth angering our lords and masters? Speaking of that, what are we doing exactly?"

"*We* aren't doing anything." My hand presses hard into the rock as I quicken my step enough to overtake the male. "I'll take it from here. You need to go back to the Academy, Tye."

Tye steps along with me. "I've been told I'm good company."

"I've been told that getting tossed into a lake will teach me to swim—that didn't make it true." I stop, turning toward him. "Why are you helping me? In fact, how did you find me near that oak to begin with?"

Tye chuckles. "You had the look of someone about to make a jailbreak. As to why I came—I'm trying to impress you, of course." He stretches. "And because it seems an entertaining way to spend the night."

"And if we are caught?"

"Then the night will quickly become less entertaining." He motions toward the passage. "Come along, mischief. You won't find the exit without me."

Fair point. Quitting arguing lest I win, I follow Tye along the uneven dips and rises until he finally blocks my path with his arm. Ordering me to stay put, the male feels along the wall until finally tugging on something I can't see. A moment later, a rope ladder unfurls beside us. Why couldn't the veil amulet have endowed me with this knowledge?

Sending me up ahead of him, Tye brings up the rear until we emerge into the wilderness. Fresh air fills my nose and lungs, washing away the stench of mold and dung my fae senses absorbed too clearly in the passage. Against the starlit sky, Tye's silhouette has a soft, preternatural glow that turns his lithe movements into dance-like perfection. Now, like me, the male stands with his face tipped up, drawing gulps of crisp air. "Where to now?"

16

LERA

"That somewhat depends on where we are," I mutter, turning about to get my bearings. The forbidding tower of the Academy's keep, the jagged mountain range, the sloping forested ridge, all stand mocking sentinel against the night. Clear, yet telling me nothing. When I approached the Academy, the damn stone relic was rather proactive in attracting my attention, but my secret hopes that its shards might oblige me with the same courtesy are fading quickly. Which means I am going to be looking for my own tracks in the forest after all. A fool's errand at night. My feet trip over a root I'd failed to notice, the loud crackle of dry leaves and branches as I fumble for balance a mockery in itself.

Stars. A heaviness settles on my chest, the weight of it making it hard to inhale. What the bloody hell was I thinking coming out here? Dragging Tye right along into trouble with me? Tye, who thinks he is human and me no more than a conquest. A distraction. My fingers grip my shirt hem as I turn about, the forest alive with an owl's ghostly hoots and a wolf's too-close howl. Just like Shade, except not. A tremor runs through me.

Everything is *just like* but not. What if this is the reality, and the soul-gripping connection I thought I had with the males was never anything but a trick of magic? If we were truly meant for each other, would they not have noted me? Felt something? Anything? The wind blows into my face, its icy fingers racing down my skin. If this is the truth of it without magic helping us, then breaking the amulets' hold heralds nothing but pretty lies. My throat closes, my eyes stinging, though I don't let the tears fall.

"Lass?" Tye's hands settle on my shoulders, turning me toward him.

I swallow, suddenly unsure what to do. What to say. Five. There are supposed to be five of us. And now there aren't. And it hurts like a knife slicing across my soul.

"Five what?" Tye asks, and I realize I've spoken the word aloud. "What are you searching for, Lera?"

"Tracks," I say numbly. "I dropped something on my way. I'd hoped to find it."

"At night?"

"I couldn't exactly walk out during daylight, now could I?"

Tye's answering chuckle vibrates through me, a rumble that starts in his chest and makes my bones tremble. Alone in the darkness with nothing but the sounds of the forest around us, the deep loneliness I've somehow held at bay before now slams into me with a bitter vengeance. Before I can draw my next breath, Tye pulls me in against his shoulder, his arms wrapping me tightly, his heart a steady beat beneath his breast. His fresh scent is a balm to my senses, his muscles surrounding me like steel wrapped in velvet.

The phantom limb of magic that I awoke with in this new fae body stirs in its shackles, unable to move.

I want him. Every fiber in my body wants to be pressed against his, even with the mating bond muted. I may not be his female right now, but he is my male. And I'm too lonely, too tired, to care about the former.

My hand fists in Tye's shirt, pulling the male toward me roughly, my lips covering his with desperate need. As the warrior's taste fills me, his achingly familiar mouth hot against mine, my body wakens, begging for more. Real or not.

Tye's hands grip either side of my face, pulling me away gently even as his sudden hardness throbs against my belly. His breath comes hard, his green eyes gleaming in the moonlight. "Not that I mind, lass, but I think you do. Or will come morning."

My heart pounds against my ribs, the sound echoing in my ears. "Come morning, I'll deny it ever happened," I say, my breath ragged. Needy. Maybe I'm not Tye's conquest, but he is mine. A notch on *my* damn belt. My teeth grind together, my hands digging into his shoulders. "Don't go getting attached, pretty lad."

A tiny predatory growl escapes Tye's lips, his emerald eyes flashing in the moonlight. "Oh, we'll see about the morning, lass. I'm told I can be *very* memorable." The male's mouth is descending upon mine even as he bites off his own words, his body pushing me back back back until I feel a tree trunk digging into my shoulders.

Tye's kiss deepens, his lips and tongue plundering my mouth with hot savageness. Heat ripples through my core, my legs and arms and abdomen tingling with energy as pressure builds high between my thighs. My sex pulses hungrily, blindly. More. I want more. The void inside me howls, screaming for Tye's cock while I clench and clench around nothing.

With a growl, I shove into Tye, my strength too great to be mortal even in this world's shackles. A lesser male would have swayed from the assault, but Tye, Tye only lifts his face away from mine as his body absorbs everything I can throw and doesn't give an inch. Heartbeat after heartbeat, he stands his ground, looming over me while his broad shoulders block out the moonlight. He stands, taking it all—until he moves.

Grabbing my wrists, he pins them above my head, his knee forcing my thighs apart. Deprived of means to squeeze my legs, the pressure along my sex turns unbearable. I struggle futilely against his hold, each failed attempt to escape only feeding the merciless ache inside me.

A flash of Tye's teeth, of the canines I can't see, and a sharp sting sinks into the tender spot where my neck and shoulder meet. The pain of the claiming shoots down my body, turning to exquisite heat.

Tye licks the bite, the tiny laps of his tongue starkly soft, as exotic as ice in the eye of a flame. I writhe, but the iron bands of his hands at my wrists let me do nothing but feel every unbearable zing. My body trembles, the surrender and storm of sensation battering me from all sides. The world about me narrows to the dampness soaking my underthings, to the tingling heat that brings me to my toes with desperation.

Tye shifts my wrists until he controls both my arms with one hand, his other sliding along my shoulder, my breast, my waist and *down down down*.

17

RIVER

*C*oal tapped his ear, signaling to River.

River paused, cocking his head in search of the sound that Coal had marked. A wolf howled. An owl hooted nearby, a pair of squirrels who should be sleeping scattering along the trees instead. As if something—someone—was disturbing their slumber. Someone whose heavy breathing River could now make out.

A small movement of River's hand had Coal walking again, the warrior's steps silent on the cold earth. A predator stalking prey. River's steady heartbeat kept its rhythm even as his mind raced. Whatever the foe, it was too close to the Academy. Had to be put down. Now. Tonight. With Shade's help if possible, but not at the risk of letting it escape. River's blade whispered free of its sheath.

The sounds of panting breath increased, branches

snapping beneath feet that belonged to neither River nor Coal. Close enough to the Academy's wall that a stone's throw would reach it. Stopping with his back pressed against a wide oak that was the last point of concealment between them and the target, River shared a readying glance with Coal.

The warrior nodded.

River's hand lifted and closed into a fist in the moonlight. *Go. Go. Go.*

Twisting around the trunk at the same time as Coal, River brought his sword into ready guard just as the foliage opened to—

Tyelor of Blair, pinning Leralynn of Osprey to a bloody oak, the man's hand so deeply inside the woman's tight pants that his fingers couldn't help but be stroking inside her hot folds even now.

River's chest tightened, heat simmering in his blood and filling his lungs, his face, his hands. Leralynn's auburn hair was loose but for a single braid on the left side, swinging like a mesmerizing pendulum with the couple's movement. The moonlight showed the naked skin of her exposed throat as she tilted up her head to meet Tye's kiss, her undulating body giving so generously of itself that a tremor ran along River's skin, making his cock twitch at the thought.

The furnace inside River blazed hotter with each of Lera's soft gasps, and when her face turned slightly, she reminded him so much of Diana that River had to bite back a roar. The damn woman was out in the wilderness, beyond the Academy's protective walls, here where three people had died in as many nights. That alone made River's arms long to shake her. Except his arms wanted to do so much more than just shake the woman. The scent of her arousal spun River's head, the glistening wetness on Tye's fingers as his hand slowly withdrew and slid up her torso toward her heavy breasts as tantalizing as chilled wine in a desert's midst. An ache he had no right to feel for a student gripped River's groin so fiercely that no shifting would be enough to relieve the sudden horrid tightness in his britches.

"What the bloody hell are you two doing?" River's voice was ice. Too controlled for his racing heart, so polar to the inferno inside him that it was a wonder the two didn't meet in an eruption of steam.

Lera gasped, tearing her mouth away from Tye's.

Tye cursed, his green-eyed gaze moving between River and Coal in a too-experienced assessment of the situation even as he pushed Leralynn behind him. As if his back would protect the woman from the deserved wrath.

Leralynn's eyes widened as she met River's, her skin blanching beautifully. When she turned, River caught sight of the sword hilt rising above her shoulder. She'd not come here just for the...for companionship, then. River didn't know whether that made him feel better or worse.

Not that it mattered. Leralynn was done. Sage might not allow students to be shown the door outright, but by the time River was through with her, she'd be running for the exit. Which would be best for all involved.

LERA

I gasp. My body, trembling in anticipation of the release Tye's deft fingers teased to the surface so skillfully, recoils at the abrupt change.

River's ire saturates the air, overpowering the forest's fresh scent. Sheer masculine dominance in each contour of his muscular body, his movements vibrate with a restrained violence that—despite my wishes—stokes my anxiety and arousal in equal measure. I focus on the chill breeze to clear my foggy mind. River is angry, yes, but it is a kind of fury I'd imagine the male reserves for an invading host from the dark realm, not a stray student snogging in the darkness. As it is, the intensity in River's gray gaze is so potent, his eyes seem to glow with it.

A few paces away, Coal stands with his arms crossed over his chest.

I've been here before, between an angry River and

glaring Coal, and a contrite Tye. But as familiar as it is—as they are—the alien coldness in their eyes is a harsh reality.

Tye shifts his weight, placing himself in the line of fire between River and me, but I need not look at River again to know there will be no reprieve. For whatever reason, the male's attention is locked on me alone, and only I can decide whether to answer the challenge or crumple beneath it.

My chin rises. My breaths, rapid after Tye's deft touch, escape in small puffs of steam. Meeting River's eyes, I match him glare for glare as his command of the forested alcove, the Academy, the very air around us ripples out with absolute certainty. His command of everything—except me.

Crossing the two paces between us, River pushes Tye aside to grab my chin between thumb and forefinger. The movement sings with the self-confidence of the king River doesn't remember he is. The veil amulet might confuse the memories, but it plainly leaves the essence of soul and experience intact. Except River's soul now finds mine a stranger.

I pull back.

"Stand still, Cadet." River injects the entire ocean of difference between our statuses into those three words. "I inquired what you are doing here—in explicit violation of the rules—one day after your arrival."

"I brought her here, sir," Tye drawls with just enough impertinence to give River no choice but to turn some of his wrath toward the male. Once assured of River's attention, Tye pulls his shoulders back farther, raising his head in a gesture that exposes his neck more than offers a challenge. "Leralynn is an attractive woman, and I had hoped the spice of...the forbidden forest might give me the advantage I need to secure her affections. Or at least her consent."

"It is fortunate that that spice also enticed the young woman in question to bring a sword." Stepping out of the woods, Shade surveys the four of us. The male's yellow eyes are so familiar that I can't help but hold my breath in anticipation of recognition, of his long arms wrapping around my body, cocooning me in their tender warmth.

A kernel of hope rises inside me. We are a quint, strongest when together. Now that the five of us are so close...

Shade's yellow eyes trace the outline of my body before focusing on my face. His full lips open. Shut. Shaking himself, he drags his gaze back toward River. "I think I found at least one of our wild beasts. And before you ask, there won't be time to get Tyelor and his... companion...back behind the wall. The wind's been carrying our scent to it, not the other way around. Anyone with a weapon should pull it now."

I draw my sword. In my side vision, Coal nods approvingly, reaching down into his boot to toss a knife to Tye—the only one of us still unarmed. I feel the twin to Coal's knife in my own boot, my hands aching to draw it. But I fight better with one weapon, and whatever is coming already has Shade bringing his blade to ready guard.

The trees rustle, and a familiar snort-like breathing now reaches my ears. A few moments later, not even our upwind position can mask the stench-filled calling card of the dark realm's rodent—not that the males remember how to interpret the smell. I brace myself for the sclices, but when three dark shapes leap at us from the darkness, I find myself unable to focus, my gaze sliding off the shapes as if trying to grip grease.

Tye stumbles beside me, blood flowing from his shoulder as he shoves a shape away. A heartbeat later, a blow I don't see coming knocks me flat onto the earth, droplets of yellow saliva streaking across my face.

I kick away the shape I can't focus on. It yields. The sclice is lighter than I'm used to. Certainly smaller than the one who tagged my ribs back in Slait. For a heartbeat, I see the rodent before me—a scrawny elongated hog beast with a too-large lower jaw even by sclice standards. Then the heartbeat is gone, my gaze skidding away from the dark shape as the amulet around my neck heats, scalding my skin.

Stars. I freeze halfway to my feet. The veil amulet. The bloody amulet that I can't take off in front of anyone here, lest they haul me to a prison cell or worse. Leralynn of Osprey, the human, does not see the sclices—but Lera of Lunos sees them just fine.

LERA

*R*iver grabs my waist, pushing me behind him as he crouches into a fighting stance.

"Don't trust your eyes," Coal orders, his voice low and level and so calm that I'd never think him playing with death if I wasn't looking at it now. His eyes closed, cheekbones and jaw sharp in the moonlight, Coal dances with his sword, the pattern making the most of his prowess and immortal senses. "The beasts play tricks with the darkness."

The beasts play tricks with your mind.

Still in front of me, River crouches, his head cocked in concentration before he strikes with his sword and dark blood spills onto the ground, the stench of it enough to make me gag. Now that I know what I should be looking at, I can make out the shapes again. Three snarling slices with vertical-slitted eyes and back-hinged knees and too-long front limbs—all familiar, yet off. The one River just wounded is too tall but scrawny, while the one about to fall to Coal's sword has so many fangs that its mouth looks to be permanently hinged open. My head pulses with the effort of watching them against the insistence of my amulet that I look away. The moment I relax my concentration, my gaze slips. It is as if these perverted versions of sclices have a crude veil of their own and the only reason my fae self can see them is because I already know what they are.

Branches crack behind me, the sounds as loud as thunder in the darkness. I jerk around so quickly that the earth sways, my mind groping for the slipping focus, without which I see nothing of the sclices. *Too long.* I've waited too long to strike, making myself vulnerable. I give up straining my mind in favor of swinging my sword in a full wide circle.

I hit only air.

My stomach squeezes, my hands white-knuckled around my sword. The sclice is close. So very close. My heart races. I swing again. Blindly. Wildly. Losing my footing for lack of contact.

As I stumble, a hog's rancid breath brushes the back of my neck.

Before I can scream, a great wolf leaps from the woods, his yellow eyes flashing as he throws himself onto the shape behind me. Gray fur and darkness roll, dragging one another back into the forest's shadows.

"Shade!" I call after him, my voice cracking from my too-dry mouth.

A few paces off, Coal grunts with satisfaction as his sword finds its mark and a sclice tumbles to the ground, its body and dull dead eyes suddenly visible. "What the bloody hell is this?" Coal rolls the corpse over with his foot.

"Something damned by the fae," says River.

I cringe—and not just from River's words. Sclices are ugly enough, but deformed ones are worse still. Now that I can see it clearly, the beast's corrupt mouth takes up half its face, the saliva rolling free from the hideous maw. From beneath the short fur hide, the sclice's skin protrudes in a mosaic of moles, one so large, it looks like a warped snowflake.

I turn away from the corpse, my chest tight as I take in the settled silence. With the dead body at Coal's feet, I hear no more movement. The males, their swords at the ready, disperse toward the edges of the clearing to check for additional intruders, their beautiful faces tight with concentration. Feeling. Listening. Scenting—for whatever good that will do with the whole place reeking of sewage.

I shake myself, a tingle along my spine screaming that the males are wrong. I saw three of the beasts, which means one is still *here*. Staying still. Lying in ambush. Forcing my breath and heart to slow, I survey the battleground, my mind on nothing but the truth of the sclice's existence. *I am Lera of Lunos. I am not human.* The amulet burns against my skin, the headache returning. *I am Lera of Lunos. I*—I gasp as red-slitted eyes crouched low beneath a bush not a pace away meet mine.

Thick-as-tree-trunk limbs, a melon-sized snout, teeth made to shred meat. *Bloody stars.*

The discovered sclice roars, rushing me just as I raise my sword. Dark blood sprays the air.

"Not bad for a wee lass," Tye mutters at the edge of my hearing.

"Not bad for a damn soldier," Coal echoes, with equal quiet. "But could be better."

My arms tremble from the strain. Even with my blade solidly striking flesh, the sheer size and force of the beast brings me to my knees. My breath catches, my lungs too tight to draw air.

The wounded sclice rears to its full height looming over me, clawed limbs ready to tear.

Everything inside me screams to roll away, to sprint, to run run run. I force my hands to stay on the sword. With my heart and breath speeding, it won't be long until I can't focus enough to see the sclice anymore—and the males are blind to it utterly. I have to stay, to drive the sword firmly into the beast's flesh. Not a killing blow—I've struck the thing's thigh—but a way to mark the sclice's location for the others. Give my males a chance.

The raised claws lower. My ribs scream in anticipated pain of another sclice attack, my body readying itself for the blow. With all the muscle I've ever gained, I force the blade in in in.

Something rips me away just before the sclice's nails

rake the space where my head was. Iron-hard arms, pounding heart, a scent of fury and woods. The male gripping me twists in the air, taking the brunt of our fall against a wedge of stump and stones.

"Have you no sense?" River shouts into my face, his eyes surveying me desperately. Pushing off the ground, he hauls me upright, the hands he had around my waist now gripping my shoulders. "You could have died just now, Leralynn." He shakes me, his eyes flashing. "Do you understand?"

"Yes," I breathe. In my side vision, I see Coal and Tye's twin assaults converging on the sword I've left in the sclice—the blade now appearing to fly about in the darkness. A heartbeat later, the outline of a too-large sclice drops to the ground, becoming more and more visible as dark liquid drains from its severed neck. Coal spares me a brief nod of approval before cleaning off his blade.

Safe. We are all safe. Relief slams into me so powerfully that I stumble, only River's grip on my shoulders holding me up. River. Right. I look back into his ice-gray eyes, recalling the question. "Yes, sir."

He lets me go too quickly, hollering for Shade as he surveys the new kill.

"I'm here." Shade—once again in his fae form—steps out of the woods where his wolf disappeared minutes earlier, breathing hard. I wonder what would have happened if the males saw Shade shift before their very eyes—and whether it is better or worse that they didn't. Of the four, Shade and Tye are the only shifters, though

Tye's relationship with his tiger is very tenuous still. If *that* shift happened in the mortal world, all hell would break lose.

My attention focuses on Shade, my heart squeezing at the beautiful sight of him, his swinging black hair, damp with sweat, his arms rippling with corded muscle. Shade exchanges curt nods with Coal—who is now clearing the perimeter—before jogging to River. "I took one down, whatever it was. How did you make out?"

I step forward despite myself, my soul calling toward the shifter. "The wolf—"

Tye gives me an odd look.

"Wolf?" Shade glances my way, his yellow eyes slightly unfocused, as if struggling to orient. "No. Whatever it was, it was no wolf."

My breath stops. Shade thinks I'm asking about the sclice he killed. Shade doesn't know he shifted. Doesn't realize his wolf was involved in the tussle. Neither does *anyone*, it seems. Surely they'd remember… Unless the veil covered up the too-close shift by distracting the males' attention from the wolf altogether. Given that the animal was among us for mere heartbeats, it's possible. I swallow. Given what's already happened with the amulet's powerful magic, anything is bloody possible.

"No, that is certainly not a wolf," Coal says, jerking his head toward the sclice corpses. "I've no notion what it is, but 'deranged hog' seems descriptive enough."

"Are you all right, lass?" Tye's voice brushes the top of my head, and I realize the male has come up behind me, his feet as silent as a tiger's. Warm callused hands brush along my shoulders and arms, the touch so familiar, I want to burrow in Tye's chest.

"It appears we found your mystery beasts, River," Shade mutters nearby, his face pulled back in a grimace. "So the night wasn't wasted, at least."

I close my eyes. Not *River's* mystery beast—the Academy's. This perverted trio of sclices had been killing for a week before we stepped foot on Great Falls grounds, and would have gone on doing so if not for us. *Us*—the quint. Whether the males know it or not, we are where we are supposed to be.

Tye's cheek presses against my hair. "Did you know you smell of lilac?" he drawls softly.

"Your shoulder—" I open my eyes, remembering the blood from the initial contact, and reach for the male.

"Shade." River's ice-cold voice cuts between us before I can touch Tye, the command in it instantly summoning everyone's attention. "Please examine Tyelor while Coal escorts Leralynn back to the Academy and places her chambers under guard. I will deal with them both tomorrow."

As Coal's callused fingers encircle my arm firmly, his familiar metallic scent surrounding me, I give one last glance at the shattered clearing, three precious males cleaning up with the calm practicality of seasoned warriors. And then, with a small shift of his face toward me, all I can see are River's furious gray eyes. Lingering in my mind long after the night swallows them.

<The End>

CONTINUE the GREAT FALLS ACADEMY adventure with episode 2, Crime and Punishment

---

Reviews are a book's lifeblood. If you enjoyed this episode, please consider saying a few words about it on Amazon. Even a single sentence helps a lot!

TRACING SHADOWS

UNRAVELING DARKNESS

TILDOR

THE CADET OF TILDOR

SIGN UP FOR NEW RELEASE NOTIFICATIONS at https://
links.alexlidell.com/News

ABOUT THE AUTHOR

Alex Lidell is an Amazon KU All Star Top 50 Author Awards winner (July, 2018). Her debut novel, THE CADET OF TILDOR (Penguin, 2013) was an Amazon Breakout Novel Awards finalist. Her Reverse Harem romances, POWER OF FIVE and MISTAKE OF MAGIC, both received Amazon KU Top 100 awards for individual titles.

Alex is an avid horseback rider, a (bad) hockey player, and an ice-cream addict. Born in Russia, Alex learned English in elementary school, where a thoughtful librarian placed a copy of Tamora Pierce's ALANNA in Alex's hands. In addition to becoming the first English book Alex read for fun, ALANNA started Alex's life long love for fantasy books. Alex lives in Washington, DC.

Join Alex's newsletter for news, special offers and sneak peeks: https://links.alexlidell.com/News

Find out more on Alex's website: www.alexlidell.com

SIGN UP FOR NEWS AND RELEASE NOTIFICATIONS

Connect with Alex!

www.alexlidell.com

alex@alexlidell.com

Printed in Great Britain
by Amazon

43894867R00088